BLACK QUIET

TED GALDI

AETHON THRILLS

aethonbooks.com

BLACK QUIET
©2023 TED GALDI

1

Cole Maddox is dressed as a waiter even though he is not one. He is a black-ops commando in Delta Force, an elite unit of the US Army.

"Champagne?" He presents a tray of glasses to a female guest at a hundred-person bash at a villa in Mykonos, Greece owned by Feng Liao, a tech billionaire from China.

The pretty, twentysomething brunette bites her lip as she takes in thirty-five-year-old Cole's well-defined facial features, dirty-blond hair, and fit body, six foot two, about two hundred pounds.

"Sure," she says. "Have one with me out on the balcony?"

He passes her a glass. "The drink is a la carte. Don't take it personally. Not looking to get fired."

She runs a finger from her eye down her cheek like a tear.

He grins, then turns his back to her and progresses toward Feng, who stands near the DJ booth in a well-tailored suit. Feng admires his crowd, most of it female European models half his age. Two slide their hands over each other's bodies as they dance in front of him to the pulsing electro music.

A special glass on Cole's tray is reserved for Feng. According to the NSA's monitoring of his communications the last three months, Feng is plotting a cyberattack on the US power grid later this week. Thousands of American injuries and deaths are expected in the resultant mayhem.

Cole gives glasses to guests. Just two are left on his tray once he arrives at Feng. "Champagne?" Cole asks.

He knows Feng wants some before he answers. The drink is his favorite according to the surveillance Cole conducted on him this last week.

"Certainly," Feng says. "Thank you, sir."

Cole's hand reaches for the reserved glass. But another hand snatches it. A blond girl holds it above her head, her eyes closed as she gyrates to the music.

"Excuse me, miss," Cole says, with Feng close enough to overhear.

She opens her eyes and lifts the glass toward her lips.

Cole grips it before she sips. "That one is flat."

"Nah-ah. Look at the cute little fizz."

"You can use even more cute little fizz." He sets the glass back on the tray and hands her the other. "This'll be better. I promise."

His gaze stretches across the roomful of dancing girls and lavish decor to Trent Winters, a fellow undercover commando working the bar. Trent slipped a tasteless, dissolvable pill into the special glass, a military-lab-engineered poison that'll kill whoever ingests it within four hours.

The commandos communicate with each other without words, just subtle signals:

Cole scratches his cheek, meaning *No go.*

Trent scratches his ear: *Let's regroup.*

Cole runs a hand through his hair: *Okay.*

He says to Feng, "I'll grab you a fresh one. Hang tight." He turns to the bar.

"I must admit," Feng says, "I agree with Sophia." Cole looks back at him. Feng points at the lone glass on the tray. "It doesn't appear flat."

"Not by normal standards. But only the best for top clients like you, Mister Liao."

"I don't recognize you from my last event. Usually the firm sends the same help."

"Service industry. High turnover." Cole grins.

"One last thing."

Cole faces him again.

"My friend is a licensed sommelier," Feng says. "I'd like him to inspect that glass. We just uncorked its bottle. If a serving went flat already, even slightly so, we may have a broader problem with the case. Which was not cheap." He raises his arm with a half-spin of his hand.

Within seconds, a brawny Asian man appears at his side, the collar of his dress shirt tight around his muscular neck. The subtle bulge of a shoulder-harness pistol is under his suit jacket.

Feng fills him in on the champagne predicament. The bodyguard nods a couple times, then says to Cole, "Maybe it's flat, maybe not. Only one way to find out."

"That so?"

"A taste test." He plucks the glass off the tray, extends it to Cole. "You go first. Let me know what you think. Then I'll have a taste and provide my opinion."

"I prefer beer."

"Just a sip should suffice. Please."

Feng must fear the US government is on to him and warned his bodyguard about possible threats from strangers at this party.

Cole looks at the Mediterranean Sea out the big window, streaked with the oranges of a late-afternoon July sun. He decides he'll have to complete this mission the old-fashioned way.

"All right, one sip," he says, accepting the glass. "Bottoms up."

He lifts it toward his lips, then releases it and the tray and slugs the bodyguard in the bridge of the nose.

The beefy guard totters backward and bangs into the DJ booth. A speaker falls, a warped sound to the music. Nearby females scream.

Feng dashes to the front door. Cole eyes Trent between the heads of gawking girls and shouts, "Door."

Trent maneuvers through the crowd to the home's entrance. Feng adjusts course, darting to a staircase in the foyer.

Cole sprints after him. He glances over his shoulder, the bloody-faced bodyguard staggering to his feet, reaching under his jacket. He unsheathes his pistol. Cole picks up a girl in the line of fire.

Bachaw. The sound of a gunshot as Cole dives into the foyer with her, corkscrewing through the air. His back hits the marble floor, the bullet zipping above them, shattering a glass vase.

"Leave the house," Cole tells the shrieking girl. In his right periphery, Feng climbs the stairs to the second level. In his left periphery, the armed guard approaches.

Cole grabs the circular granite table the broken vase is on and angles it in front of him like a shield.

Bachaw. The table shakes as a bullet strikes it, a chunk chipping off onto the floor.

With the table in front of his face and torso, Cole backpedals up the stairs after Feng. Another bullet rattles the granite. In a large mirror in the high-ceilinged foyer, he spots the bodyguard pursuing him, tilting his gun downward, lining up a shot at Cole's exposed legs.

Cole waits for his pistol to steady, then jumps. A round flies under him into the staircase. Airborne, Cole chucks the fiftyish-pound table at his opponent. It smashes his chest. The guard's back thwacks the hardwood steps. The table lands on his face, crushing his skull. His limbs inert, he flops to the marble floor.

Cole spins, rushes up the remaining stairs. At the far end of the second-level hallway, Feng disappears through a doorway. Cole races to it.

Handle locked. He kicks it, the brass knob snapping off. He shoulders open the door.

The master bedroom. Feng at a night table, a pulled-out drawer, little beeps as if from a gun safe's electronic keypad.

Cole charges at him. Feng turns with a pistol in his hand. He aims it.

Cole bats down Feng's wrist. The weapon goes off, a round blowing through the ornate area rug. Cole's shoulder drives into Feng's stomach, knocking him into the night table. Its lamp topples to the floor beside the wrestling men.

On his back, Feng re-aims the weapon. Before he can squeeze the trigger, Cole grabs the top of Feng's head with one hand, his chin the other, and rips his neck into an unnatural position. Cole hears a sound like the crack of a thick twig.

Footsteps by the bedroom doorway. Trent emerges with the dead guard's gun. He eyeballs Feng's corpse and nods at Cole, who's digging his hand into Feng's pockets. He finds his cell-phone, a potential source of intel on coconspirators.

The two US operatives tear off their white waiter shirts, revealing yellow tee shirts. Trent barricades the doorway with the dresser while Cole pulls the sheet off the bed, rolls it up, and ties an end around the headboard. He and Trent descend through a window to the backyard, using the sheet like a rope, and jog off the property to the extraction van.

2

Cole hammers a stake in his brother's backyard to be used for games of horseshoes once company arrives. Though the sun shines, the early-October Montana air has a bite to it, chilling his face.

Powaw, Cole's adoptive father, situates chairs around a folding table with pink *Happy Birthday* balloons in the center. He's thin with long, black hair. The seventy-three-year-old Native American is a retired carpenter in the brothers' family's construction company.

"Son," Powaw says.

Cole stops hammering. "Yeah?"

Powaw waves him over. "I've been so happy you're back home to stay, I couldn't help but make you something." From his pocket he pulls out a bracelet, about two dozen black beads and one red. "It represents the red wolf." He points at Cole's heart. "The spirit inside you."

"It's beautiful. I don't know what to say."

"Say nothing. Put it on."

Cole slips it around his wrist and grins.

A Chevy pickup edges into view on the street, a metallic

speck among the ponderosa pine-covered Montana mountaintops towering above it. It zips toward the quaint brown house well above the speed limit.

The truck parks in the driveway and, within two seconds, Cole's older brother Jay pops out, thirty-eight, five foot seven, pudgy in the waist and cheeks. He wears paint-splattered work boots and a dusty *Maddox Construction* sweatshirt.

He says to Cole and Powaw, "Thanks for setting up." He fishes a dinosaur costume out of his backseat. "As I'm putting in drywall, I get a call from the party agency. The girl who was supposed to play Princess Petunia came down with strep throat this morning. They had nobody else available on short notice, but let me borrow a getup for Timmy Tyrannosaurus." He holds the small green leotard up with an anxious expression.

Cole laughs. "I'd go easy on the burgers if you want to fit in that thing, bud. FYI, I just barbecued three dozen, put them on the counter inside with a couple big bowls of chips and pretzels."

"And I picked up the ice and beer," Powaw says. "Filled up two coolers on the deck."

Jay gives them an appreciative bow and hustles to the house's sliding-glass back door. His wife Melanie opens it, thirty-two, honey-colored hair. Their one-year-old daughter Quinn, in her arms, wears a *Birthday Girl* shirt.

Melanie kisses Jay. "Hey hon. How'd the job go?"

"Good. But I stink a little."

She sniffs him. "Affirmative."

"Let me take a quick shower before everyone shows up." He squeezes Quinn's cheeks. "Look at this cuteness. It's just ridiculous."

Melanie slaps his butt as he scurries into the house, then walks down a few steps to the backyard and flashes Cole and Powaw a thumbs-up. "Great work, men."

Soon Jay emerges in the dinosaur costume, the green spandex

straining against his thighs and stomach. Baby Quinn giggles and claps.

"I need a shot of you guys," Cole says, pulling his phone from his pocket. "Mel, get in there." She sidles up to Jay with the baby. Cole snaps the picture. "Ah, it's perfect. I'll text it to you." He turns to Powaw, who favors physical photos. "And I'll get a copy printed for you, Pop."

Powaw nods.

In a couple minutes the guests begin pouring into the back-yard with presents. Cole sees thirties' versions of a few teenage faces he recalls from the halls of Timber Ridge High School. These former acquaintances are happy to see him, and he them.

One guy, of course, brings up the revered local incident known as "The Jump." Cole, at twelve, rode his bike off a cliff up at Larkspur Mountain, sailing over a wide gap in the terrain with a hundred-foot drop before landing on the other side. At the time, he was the only known person, kid or adult, to attempt the feat and, according to his old pal, still is.

A face turns the corner with more memories attached to it than the others combined. Heather. Cole's high school girlfriend. Her green eyes meet his from across the yard. She is still as beautiful as she was then.

"Oh my God," she says, noticing him. "Mel told me you're finally back from the oil rig. I was hoping to see you today."

"Yeah, I'm learning the ropes at the family company now. I was glad to hear you were coming to the party."

Cole earned a football scholarship to play tight end for the University of Montana, where Heather went, but turned it down. He still remembers breaking her the news, the eighteen-year-old her crying on the bathroom floor of her parents' house. Back then, he knew college wasn't for him, but wasn't certain what he wanted to do with his life.

He traveled the US for a year working odd jobs before

enlisting in the military. Once he was recruited into black ops, he needed a cover story, so told people back in Timber Ridge he was a safety inspector on an oil rig. Only Powaw, Jay, and Melanie know the truth of his past.

"Ever pursue interior design?" he asks Heather.

"Got my own firm going on seven years now."

"Nice. I remember how good your paintings from art class were. Especially that one you did of Jackrabbit Canyon Lake they hung in the cafeteria. I would point it out to my friends when we walked by."

A man in khakis and a checkered sweater paces up to her, holding the hand of a girl about six. A ring on his finger. Heather's too.

Cole extends his hand to him. "Hey, I'm Cole."

The man shakes it. "Gabe."

"Great to meet you, Gabe."

Heather taps the little girl's back. "And this is Jenny."

Blushing, the child looks at the ground. Cole kneels, his eyeline level with hers. He grins and says, "Hi Jenny. I like your cool hair ribbon."

"Danks."

A tinge of sadness in him. If he accepted that scholarship and dated Heather through college, they would've wound up engaged and an adorable little girl like this could've been his today. Being single and childless never bothered him in the army. But, for some reason, pokes at him now.

"We've got food inside," he says, standing. "If you guys aren't in the mood for burgers, let me know and I can throw chicken or hot dogs on the grill."

He waves and drifts to the deck, where he pulls a Coors Light bottle from a cooler. Sipping it, he watches a few parents and their kids in a three-legged race.

"Snag me one of those bad boys," Jay says through the

dinosaur mask. He takes it off, a film of sweat on his forehead. "This thing is like a Russian sauna."

Cole smiles and passes him a beer. "Want to watch the baseball playoff tonight at my place?"

Jay twists off the bottle cap and swigs. "Yeah, but I might be late. Gotta fix a lady's drying machine on Lenkil Ave after the party."

"Another side gig?"

"Things were rough out there for a while after the Hadaway factory shut down. Taking anything I can get. Saving for college is expensive." Jay pats Cole on the back. "I've got the situation under control, though."

Situation implies immediate circumstances that need fixing, while funding a college account is a long-term activity. A strange comment. But Cole doesn't want to pry.

"Me versus you in horseshoes?" Cole asks.

"That depends. You ready for an ass walloping?"

Jay puts his mask back on, roars like a T-rex, and slaps Cole on the side.

Cole chuckles and slaps him back. They go back and forth trying to hit each other just like they did as young boys.

3

A heap of cedar-wood planks sits in the garage of Cole's modest cabin. According to the Native American teachings Powaw passed down, getting out on a lake in a boat and floating among the voices of animals may allow Cole to better hear his own voice, which could help with the uneasiness he's felt since leaving the army.

Cole, who's trying to transition into the construction industry, thought building a canoe would be a useful experience. The first step is assembling a strongback, a plywood platform for the cedar strips.

While he slips on a pair of canvas gloves, the thrum of an engine catches his attention.

He peeks outside. A kid zooms around on a dirt bike near the edge of the two-acre property, his yellow motocross outfit bright against the ash-colored sky. The neighbor boy. Cole's noticed him and his mom coming and going a few times. No sign of a dad ever.

The kid's helmeted head turns to Cole, then he speeds up and attempts a slanted stop. He almost tips his bike but sticks out a leg to regain his balance.

"Whoa," Cole calls out, guessing the boy is trying to impress him. "Nice move."

"Oh." The kid lifts his visor, revealing his dimpled face. "I didn't even see you there."

Cole laughs inside. The boy rides over to him. Cole pegs him as eleven.

The kid scopes the workout bench and weights inside the garage. "Rad set of iron. My mom says I'm still too young for my own. But me and my friends go in the woods sometimes and lift rocks. Nathan can do bigger ones than me. But I can beat Liam."

This kid is funny. Cole likes him.

Cole points at the dirt bike. "Know how to do a jump on that thing?"

The kid shakes his head.

"I can pack some dirt into a slope in your yard and teach you," Cole says. "Only if your mom says okay, though."

"Bet."

"On what?"

The kid chuckles. "No. It's just what you say when you're cool with something. My mom didn't know it either the first time I said it to her. Let me ask her now."

The kid guns his engine to his house and runs inside. Within a few minutes he makes his way over to Cole's on foot with his mom.

She wears a peacoat over a light-blue waitress uniform from Gold Sparrow Diner. Long black hair, full lips, and a radiant fair complexion with a dash of rosiness in her cheeks. She must've had him young. She still looks to be in her twenties.

"Hey," Cole says. "Sorry for not introducing myself till now. Moving had me occupied the past two weeks. Cole."

"I know. When I was in middle school, my parents would take me to the football games the year we won state. Lacey."

"Declan," the kid says.

"Is this jump thing Declan's talking about safe?" she asks.

"I'll start it small. Keep an eye on him. Only add height to it once he's got the fundamentals down."

She peers into Cole's face as if deciding whether to trust him. "Make sure he keeps on his helmet."

"Of course."

"I'm cooking tonight. When you're done out here, why don't you come over for dinner?"

"Appreciate it. Sure." His phone vibrates in his pocket. Melanie, his sister-in-law. "One sec," he says to Lacey, then turns his back to her and answers. "What's up?"

"Are you with your brother?" she asks, a shred of anxiety in her voice.

"No. Why?"

"He left for the drugstore about an hour ago. And never came home."

4

Cole drives his Jeep to downtown Timber Ridge. He and Melanie tried calling and texting Jay without a reply and confirmed with Powaw they're not together. Jay could've gotten a flat tire on his way back from the drugstore. Or maybe ran into a friend and became immersed in catching up.

But Cole's instincts tell him that explanation is wrong. He recalls that conversation he and Jay had on the deck three days ago at Quinn's birthday.

I've got the situation under control.

An odd statement from his brother about saving for his daughter's college fund. Jay not coming home from the drugstore and missing dinner is also odd. When two odd events occur in a row, good chance they're related.

Cole turns onto a windy road, a craggy rock face on the other side of its guardrail. In the distance, a massive shadow eclipses the abandoned building that used to be the manufacturing hub for Hadaway Outdoor Suppliers, a national brand for camping, fishing, and hunting equipment that was the economic cornerstone of Timber Ridge since the 1970s.

Last year Jay told him the factory shut down, its hundreds of jobs outsourced to Indonesia. The closure sent a debilitating ripple effect through a community with a population of only 6,500. For the first six months, Maddox Construction had almost no work. With a miniscule income during that stretch, and a new baby to pay for, Jay and Melanie lived off a credit card.

Cole rides the road down the mountain onto Main Street. Low-rise brick storefronts and free public-parking spaces line both sides. He drives past the movie theater, Marshall Cleaning and Tailoring, and a few other businesses. Though they haven't changed much since high school, what's around them has.

Back then, besides the occasional discarded soda can, the sidewalks were clean. Garbage is more prevalent now, as is the sight of homeless in tents, a probable symptom of the financial fallout from the closure of the Hadaway factory.

He notices Jay's Chevy pickup in a spot by Willard Drugs. Cole parks and peeks inside the truck. No Jay. No flat tires, no dents on the body.

He walks to Willard's, which hasn't been renovated since the 1940s. Inside are wooden shelves, a counter with red seats, a *Cold Root Beer Floats* sign. Though dated, Cole prefers it to the cold, institutional feel of many modern stores.

"How's it going?" he asks the girl at the register.

"Can I help you with something, sir?"

He scrolls through his phone's photos until locating one with Jay. The two brothers and Powaw stand at the edge of a river, each holding up a trout caught that day.

Cole zooms on Jay's face. "Did he happen to come in here recently?"

A tad of suspicion in her expression. "Why?"

Cole zooms out. "That's me with him. I'm his brother. Did you notice him talking to anyone while he was in here?"

"I see him maybe once a week. But not today. Sorry."

Her eyes hold on his, no hesitation to her voice. She doesn't seem to be lying. He taps his phone against his thigh a couple times, then slips it back in his pocket. "Thanks for your time."

"We have a special on bottled water, FYI. I'm supposed to tell everyone."

"I'm a faucet man, myself." He waves and steps outside. A crisp wind burrows under his shearling coat. A woman walks a dog. A guy turns into the tobacco shop.

Maybe Jay stopped in another store first and is still caught up inside. Cole walks the block, looking through windows for him. No sign of him anywhere.

Cole scans the sidewalk between Jay's pickup and Willard Drugs. Nothing unusual on it. An alley intersects it. At the end, three plastic trash cans are along a chain-link fence. One is toppled over. On the other side of the fence, the pavement leads to dirt. The muddy parts seem to have markings on them.

Cole climbs the fence and kneels near the mud. Shoe-sole imprints, still fresh. A men's ten, Jay's size, with the Adidas logo, Jay's preferred sneaker brand.

A second set of shoe treads are near the first, a couple sizes bigger. Both footprint patterns extend into a patch of woods about fifty feet away.

Cole follows them. The sound of the traffic on Main Street fades behind him.

He crosses into the brush, the canopy of treetops blocking out any daylight lingering in the early-evening sky. Bushes, weeds, rocks. A form lies among them that first appears like a log. Then Cole notices the sheen of a windbreaker.

He dashes to it. Jay is on his back with his arms at his sides, a gash in his forehead. Three streaks of blood ooze from it, one to his hairline, the other his nose, the other over a closed eye, across his cheek, and pooling on the ground.

Cole sticks his ear over his brother's heart. He has a pulse.

But maybe not for long.

5

The lights of an ambulance flash in the darkening sky as Jay is whisked to the emergency room. Based on Cole's look-over of the headwound, a blunt object struck his brother, fracturing his skull while tearing his flesh. Hands on his hips, Cole stands on the edge of the woods, debating what words to use when he informs Melanie and Powaw that Jay was found not just maimed, but unresponsive.

In Cole's periphery, Officer Pete Hannelson, whom he just met, addresses a trio of spectators on the other side of a yellow strip of *Crime Scene* tape. The late-twenties cop seems overwhelmed.

Hannelson, in his baggy Timber Ridge Police Department jacket, wanders back to Cole. He's short, with glasses and a light-brown bowl cut.

"Can I get you anything, Mister Maddox?" he asks. "Blanket, hot cocoa?"

"I'm okay. Thank you, though."

"We get a fair amount of complaints about the vagrants downtown. Mostly just public urination. A few muggings by addicts looking for a quick fix. Sometimes they get rough, but I've never seen one this bad."

"I told your sergeant I checked Jay's pockets after I called nine-one-one. His wallet, keys, and phone are all still there. I don't think this was a mugging."

"Huh. So he was chased through an alley, over a fence, and into the woods just to be bludgeoned in the head? Did your brother recently tick anyone off? Anyone who may've had a temper?"

"He's always had plenty of friends, rarely an enemy. No recent fights. That I'm aware of at least."

Though Cole knows what sort of man his brother is, for almost two decades they just saw each other on military breaks. Cole isn't privy to every detail of Jay's life.

The sergeant, Sandra Evans, emerges from the woods with a flashlight, early forties, stout. She holds a thermos, a cat cartoon on it beside *I'm Feline Good.*

"Anything?" Cole asks her.

"You were right, no noticeable items were left behind. But we'll get a CSI team over here to conduct a thorough search for trace evidence. Clothing fibers, hairs, bodily fluids not belonging to Jay, the kinda things hidden to the naked eye."

"That'd be great."

"You have to bear with us on the timing though. After the Hadaway factory closed and the tax base shrank, our budget was slashed. We're a bit understaffed."

"I understand." Cole points toward Main Street. "FYI, one other thing that can help. I noticed the store across the alley, Nolan Antiques, has a security camera over its front door. Some of the newer models have pretty wide fields of view. It's possible footage of the alley was captured. If so, you can hopefully see who chased Jay."

She nods. "That's absolutely right. Did you ever work in law enforcement, Mister Maddox?"

"No."

She holds her stare on him as if waiting for him to elaborate. He doesn't.

"I'll get word out to Mister Nolan about his surveillance tape tonight," she says. "Plus conduct interviews with all the employees on shift in the surrounding businesses. I'll keep you posted."

"Appreciate it, Sergeant."

"We sure appreciate you. Getting to your brother before it was too late."

She extends her hand. Cole shakes it, then Hannelson's, turns around, and paces toward his parked Jeep. A couple more onlookers linger in the alley. A hawk circles above Main.

Jay's voice echoes in Cole's head, "I've got the situation under control." His brother may have been involved in something messy. Something he hid from Cole. He may have thought he had control, but didn't.

Cole's instincts tell him to keep digging until he uncovers the truth. But he reminds himself his black-ops days are over. This investigation is not his responsibility. It's the police's. His focus right now should be on staying strong for his family.

He takes a deep breath and calls Melanie.

6

In his garage, Cole saws plywood. Outside the open door is a pre-sunrise purple sky and the black silhouettes of giant mountains. He tries to envision drifting in a canoe across a calm lake. But keeps seeing his brother's bashed-in head and hearing all the questions still unanswered.

He stacks some cedar planks on his shoulder and sprints into the woods carrying the weight. No destination in mind. His body screams for physical exertion. And he gives it to himself.

Endorphins surge through him, his sweatpants and shirt soon wicked in sweat. He runs until the sun comes up.

After a shower, he stops by Gold Sparrow Diner. Hand-painted nature scenes cover its walls.

He stares at a painted cow. He remembers being here with his biological parents one day when he was five and ordering a burger. The waiter pointed to the same cow on the wall and cracked a joke about Cole's lunch coming from it. Cole didn't get it. His mom explained that though people can love animals, they also have to kill some of them to survive. At first, Cole was horrified. Jay laughed at him. Cole's mom told him nature wanted it this way, and he was not a bad person for eating a burger.

His neighbor Lacey, pouring coffee, notices him from across the room. She approaches with a tense expression.

"My bad for bailing on dinner last night," he says. "Something came up."

"No kidding. Customers are talking about it. Your brother is apparently a beloved guy around Timber Ridge. This is just… terrible. No need to apologize. Please."

Cole looks around. A couple people stare at him while whispering to others.

"Tell Declan I didn't forget about building his ramp," he says.

"Don't worry about that right now. Your family hanging in there?"

"Last night was especially rough for my sister-in-law. I want to bring her and my pop a nice breakfast. Let's do two bagels with cream cheese and sides of bacon. And a scrambled egg burrito for me, wrapped up to stay warm if you can."

"Def."

She doesn't write the order down, instead walks up to the cook in the kitchen as if it's on priority.

Cole waits at the counter. He glimpses Lacey's interactions. Though waitressing entails a lot of stress for little pay, she does the job with zeal, gliding from table to table, putting smiles on the faces of her customers and coworkers. People here refer to her without the *y*, just *Lace*.

Once the food is ready, she refuses to accept any money from Cole. When she walks away, he still tips her, leaving a ten under a ketchup bottle. He drives to the Gallatin Health Center, an institution specializing in brain injuries in Bozeman, about an hour from Timber Ridge.

After checking in at the front desk, he walks to a waiting room. Melanie, holding Quinn, sits on a chair in sweats and Crocs. No makeup, bags under her eyes. The five other seated visitors stare at Powaw, who stands at the window, chanting at the sun under his breath.

Cole, who was taught Powaw's tribal language, understands the chant. A request to the sun for its healing powers. Cole knows to never disturb Powaw in this state, so sits beside Melanie without saying hello to his pop.

Cole holds out a Styrofoam box of food. "Thanks," she says, attempting to grab it. But she misses and it almost falls. With a groan, she takes it. She seems exhausted.

"Let me hold Quinn while you eat," he says, picking up the baby. He rests her on his chest and wraps his free arm around Melanie for a hug.

She opens the box and bites into her bagel. "I don't know how I'm going to make this place work out," she says, nodding at the sleek, modern-designed waiting room. "I get that it's the best, but our insurance plan sure isn't. Jay handles all the money stuff for us. And now I don't even have him to go to."

"You have me. Most of my savings went to buying my cabin. But I've got some left. And Pop's probably socked away a good amount over the years. Anything you need. We're here."

"Kind of you, Cole. But Jay calls that charity. He wouldn't accept it."

"It's not charity. We're family. And we're not the only ones who would help. If you set up a GoFundMe page, I'm sure dozens of people who know Jay would be happy to kick in. He's getting the best care out there."

She takes a deep breath and nods. Then lays her head on his shoulder.

Soon, the waiting room door opens. Entering is a man of average height with a familiar, handsome face. Real estate developer Wayne Shaw. He carries a gift basket, a *Get Well Soon* flag poking out the side.

Wayne must be in his early fifties, but hasn't aged much in the seventeen years since Cole's seen him, still trim, just a touch of silver on the sides of his black hair. His sweater, cowboy boots, and hat are far more stylish than any other outfit in the room.

"Cole, right?" Wayne asks with a smile. "I remember watching you play football years ago."

Cole stands with Quinn and shakes his hand. "Hi Mister Shaw."

"You're an adult now. No need to call me Mister Shaw. Wayne."

Referring to him by first name seems odd. Wayne's great-grandfather was responsible for building much of Timber Ridge. The rich Shaws are big donors to the high school's football boosters. Their company's name is painted on the back of the field's stands in larger letters than any other sponsor.

"I got to know your brother well a couple years ago," Wayne says. "Maddox Construction may be small, but works harder than anyone. Jay and his crew helped out with a few things on Valley Gate."

"Yeah, he filled me in. I drove past the development a few times. The townhouses are nice."

"Our biggest project of all time." Wayne straightens the slanting flag on his gift basket. "What room is your brother in? I want to say a prayer."

"Two forty-three. But I have to add you to a family-and-friends visitor list before they let you back. Come on."

Cole escorts him to reception and grants him approval. With a grin, Wayne heads toward the patient rooms.

Cole's phone vibrates, a call from the contact *Sgt. Sandra Evans.*

He answers. "Hey, Sergeant."

"Hello Mister Maddox. As promised, I have an update for you on the surveillance video from Nolan Antiques."

"Yes."

"Unfortunately, the alley was just out of range. A nudge to the side and we would've been able to see Jay and any likely assailant climbing that fence. I know this isn't what you were hoping to hear."

"Any other leads?"

"Nobody we interviewed downtown saw or heard anything out of the ordinary. And so far nothing turned up from the CSI squad."

Cole adjusts his grip on Quinn. "Well, if anything changes, let me know."

"Of course. I want to be honest with you, though. I'll talk to some of your brother's acquaintances to see if any evidence turns up, but I don't have the budget to put a detective on this case full time. Our best shot to find out who did this and press charges is to get a victim statement from Jay. Any sign of him waking up from the coma?"

"Not yet."

"Sorry to hear. All right, then. Until next time, Mister Maddox."

"So long."

He ends the call. The beeping of medical machinery carries through a nearby doorway. The patter of rubber soles on the linoleum floor. The voice of the receptionist. Quinn starts crying, drowning out the rest.

Though Cole hopes Jay wakes up soon, he may not. Due to Jay's lack of quality insurance, the hospital would keep him on life support for just a short period of time before letting him die. The Maddox family would of course be devastated. So would the local police's case. The perpetrator would get away with killing Jay.

Cole can't bear that possibility.

7

The garage door of Jay and Melanie's house lifts. Cole feels a bit uncomfortable snooping around here, but has to if he wants the truth.

Since Melanie slept at the hospital last night, Cole volunteered to stop here to pick up some things she can use to freshen up. She thanked him and gave him the garage code.

He enters and walks past a sign on the hallway wall with script writing, *Home Is Wherever We're Together*. A quarter-full cup of tea rests on the kitchen counter. Melanie must've been drinking it last evening and abandoned it to rush to the hospital.

He steps into the study, a framed photograph on the desk of him, Jay, and a couple of their friends at Ripsaw Mountain for a long-weekend ski trip back in high school. Jay pranked one of the guys by stuffing a fake snake under his sheets. The other three impersonated his reaction at least once an hour the rest of the trip.

Cole opens the desk's drawer. Inside is the user manual of a printer, a pen, a notepad, and in the back, a halfway-eaten bag of M&M's. Jay, a few pounds overweight, told Cole he cut out the candy. Since he was a kid, Jay has resorted to sweets in times of stress. Something must've made him cave.

Cole flips through the notepad. Dollar figures are scrawled on the most recent pages in Jay's handwriting as if he were planning out a budget. Various abbreviations are by the numbers, but Cole doesn't recognize any. Most of the dollar amounts have negative signs beside them. Jay seems to owe a lot more than he has.

Money problems can lead to bad choices. And bad choices can lead to messy predicaments like Jay's.

Cole opens the desk's Apple laptop in the hopes of learning more. The password of the computer in the Maddox Construction office is *Indy123*. Jay's favorite movie is *Indiana Jones and the Raiders of the Lost Ark*. Cole tries *Indy123* on the personal computer.

Nope.

Cole leans back in the faux-leather chair. It squeaks. If he wants to find out what's on the laptop, he'll need to bypass password entry and extract the hard drive.

That tactic is risky. If he damages it, its files can be corrupted. When the cops get around to searching the computer, they'd notice the destroyed data. Since Melanie knows Cole came here alone, the police may infer he wrecked the hard drive on purpose. He could become a suspect.

He packs a bag in Melanie's closet with clothing and toiletries, grabs the laptop, and drives to Walmart. He purchases an Apple-compatible USB SATA hard drive enclosure and goes to his cabin.

From his collection of tools in the garage, he finds a fine-tipped Phillips-head screwdriver. In his den, he flips over Jay's computer, revealing the ten tiny screws holding the back panel in place. Just before he loosens the first, his phone vibrates. A text from Melanie:

Thanks for grabbing some stuff for me but Quinn wouldn't stop crying. I'm in an Uber home with her. I'll come back later. No need for you to bring me a bag.

Not good. Cole must scrutinize the hard drive and return the computer to her study before she gets back to her house.

He rushes to remove the first screw. He sets it on his desk and starts on the second. When all ten are out, he detaches the back panel, exposing intricate components and circuitry.

With careful fingers, he unfastens the battery connector, frees the screws in the hard drive, and pulls away its bracket and tab. He lifts the rectangular object from its housing and inserts it into the enclosure he bought at Walmart.

He plugs it into his own laptop and logs into an extrapolatory software program he used in the army. It allows him to interact with someone else's hard drive as if it were his own.

Cole clicks the Safari web browser. If Jay has a financial secret, his online-banking profile will help expose it. In the URL bar, Cole enters *bank*, as in Bank of America, to see if auto-type returns any results. No. He tries *chase*, then *wells*. Yep. Wellsfargo.com was visited before with Jay's hard drive.

The browser remembers the username and password, the two fields filled in. Cole clicks *Sign On* and is directed to an overview of Jay and Melanie's checking and savings accounts. To Cole's surprise, both seem in solid shape, $3,543 in checking and $32,702 in savings.

But, as Powaw says, in rare cases does a surface tell a truth.

Cole opens ninety days' worth of checking-account transactions and sorts them by size. The largest outgoing amount is $1,221, appearing three times, to an entity called LMG Mortgage Servicing. Nothing shady about that.

He sorts the savings-account data the same way. The numbers are much plumper. On October 2 a deposit of $25,000 went into the account in cash. A few days before then, September 27, $10,000 was withdrawn, also in cash.

Cole is eager to know what his brother was doing on the days he made these big transactions. Jay's iPhone was in his pocket when the EMTs took him to the hospital. The police must have the device in evidence by now.

Though Cole doesn't possess it, he may still be able to see what's on it. iPhones pair with Apple laptops. He can view Jay's text message history from his hard drive.

Cole clicks the green-and-white *Messages* icon, pulling up the sent and received texts associated with Jay's Apple ID. He scrolls back to October 2, the day of the $25,000 deposit. Then, Jay communicated with Cole, Melanie, Powaw, Randy his high school friend, and a worker from Maddox Construction. Cole reads the exchanges. Nothing bizarre.

He scrolls back to September 27, the day of the $10,000 withdrawal. Jay messaged with Melanie, nothing suspicious, and a contact called *Flippy*. Cole reads their texts:

Flippy: *Ignatius.*

Jay: *Excellent. Thanks again man.*

They haven't texted each other since. Cole has no idea who Flippy is or what *Ignatius* means. He scrolls back to their last conversation, about a month ago:

Flippy: *Poker at my crib. 7 pm.*

Jay: *See u there.*

The week prior, Flippy sent Jay a YouTube video of a guy falling off a pogo stick. Jay replied *haha.*

The week before that:

Flippy: *Just picked up a college babe at work. She was playing mini golf in a skirt about the size of a napkin. I've still got it.*

Jay: *BS u geezer.*

Cole glimpses the clock. Twenty minutes have passed since Melanie contacted him about leaving the hospital. She can arrive home any moment.

He removes Jay's hard drive from the enclosure, situates it in the proper laptop, and secures the back panel. He gets in his Jeep and races away from his cabin.

The laptop findings swirl in his mind. He calls Powaw.

"Hi son," Powaw says. "How are you?"

"When I was overseas, did Jay ever mention a poker buddy named Flippy?"

"Why?"

"I want to talk to Jay's friends. See if they might know anything."

"Aren't the authorities doing that?"

"Maybe they missed someone. Can't hurt to hit up as many people as possible."

"It can hurt if you're trying to do the cops' job for them. If you interfere with their investigation, you can wind up in jail."

"I just want to ask some questions. Nothing major, definitely nothing illegal." Cole parks in Jay and Melanie's driveway and opens the garage.

"Your brother knows a lot of people. I'm not familiar with one called Flippy."

Cole enters the house. To his relief, Melanie isn't home yet. He places her bag in the kitchen and says into the phone, "Jay brought him up recently and I figured I'd ask. No problem."

Powaw is quiet for a while. "Rarely do I come across a man who has the spirit of the warrior wolf. But I recognized it in you the first time I took you and your brother bowhunting. A good trait, of course. But it can lead to chaos if you don't control it."

Cole sticks Jay's laptop back on the desk. "I appreciate you looking out for me. But you don't have anything to worry about."

Powaw lets out a grunt.

8

Cole paces up to a hut with *Adventure Park* on its slanted roof in big block letters. Around him are a go-kart track, a few batting cages, and mini-golf and paintball courses, reddish-brown foothills beyond them.

When Cole was a kid, his biological mom would take him here after school on his birthday to play mini-golf. After they were done, she'd have him stand by the same tree behind the last hole and scratch his height into the bark with his dad's Swiss Army knife. By the time Cole was in middle school and had a social life with friends, he outgrew the tradition.

He steps inside the pass-sales hut. Behind the counter is a sixtyish man in an Adventure Park polo.

"Howdy, young man," the attendant says with a smile.

"Morning. I'm looking for a guy I think works here. Goes by Flippy."

The attendant's smile dissolves. "If you have some issue with him, please take it up with him at his house. This is a family establishment. He's caused enough drama here."

"Just a friendly conversation is all I'm here for."

The attendant lingers for a moment, then lumbers to a radio

hanging on the wall. He says something into it out of earshot, then heads back to Cole. "Said he'll be up here in a minute."

Cole gives him an appreciative nod, then looks out the window at the park. A Wednesday morning on a school day, the target customers are in class, the batting cages empty, just two go-karts on the track, a pair of early-twenties guys laughing as they try to knock each other into the bordering orange cones.

Striding behind the batting cages is a fortysomething man in a gray jumpsuit. He's heading toward the parking lot.

Flippy is trying to ditch him.

Cole shoves open the hut's rear door and bolts outside, the noise of the go-karts becoming audible. Flippy notices him and begins sprinting.

Cole hops over the track's wall of cones.

"Watch it, dude," one of the drivers shouts, swerving around him.

Cole's arms and legs pump. Faster than Flippy, he gains ground on him. Flippy crosses onto the parking lot.

Cole hops over another wall of cones. Flippy dashes to an aging Dodge Charger. Cole can't beat him to it, so detours to his Jeep.

The Charger's engine starts. Then the Jeep's. The cars close in on the lot's exit from opposite directions. Cole yanks his wheel and slams his brake. The Jeep skids in front of the gap in the fencing, blocking the Charger from leaving.

Flippy stops short. Cole knocks on the Charger's driver's window.

Flippy rolls it down. He has a pointy face, a nervous tic to his upper lip. "If I hit on your girlfriend or something, I'm sorry."

"I'm Jay Maddox's brother."

"Oh. Shit, okay." Flippy is quiet for a bit. "I, uh, heard what happened. If you think it was me, you got the wrong guy."

"I don't think it was you. Can I come in?"

Flippy surveys his expression as if deciding whether he's a threat. Then pushes open the passenger door and says, "I've been meaning to stop by the hospital."

Cole waves at the five onlookers huddled by the track and sits in the car. "I'm trying to piece together what was going on in Jay's life the last few weeks. I get the vibe he had some pretty bad money problems. I'm asking his friends if they know anything about that."

Flippy pulls a pack of Marlboros and a lighter from the glovebox. He sparks one, sucks in a long drag. "He was looking for dough for his wife's thing. He must've told you about that though, no?"

"What thing?"

Flippy points at his eyes with his index and middle fingers, the cigarette between them. "Her, you know, condition."

"What condition?"

As Cole asks the question, he recalls Melanie's hand missing that box of breakfast in her periphery this morning. Maybe exhaustion wasn't the cause, but a vision problem. That would explain why she didn't drive to and from Bozeman herself, instead took an Uber.

"He needed to go out of pocket thirty Gs for some retina-transplant thing," Flippy says. "Shitty insurance. Your brother and his wife never even told you she had an issue?"

"If they told me, I would've insisted on pitching in for the surgery. But Jay apparently considers that charity."

"Yeah, he could be a stubborn SOB sometimes. He didn't ask me for a handout, but did come to me for…help."

"You helped him put together thirty large?"

Flippy puffs the cigarette. "I've got an in with a trainer at Expo Downs."

Cole's heard of Expo Downs, a horse-racing facility in Great Falls. "So Ignatius is a thoroughbred?"

Flippy nods.

Jay could've damaged his credit with a few late payments during the half a year with little income. If so, a big bank loan would've been difficult to obtain. In desperation, he turned to a horse race for the money. The morning of September 27, the *Ignatius* text was about a bet to place.

"Did you talk to him after he won the bet?" Cole asks. "Did anything still seem off?"

"He didn't win." Flippy's upper lip spasms. "I didn't lose as much as him that day, but I got my bell rung too. This trainer never disappointed me in the past. He's got the hush-hush on any horse coming into a race jacked up on 'roids. Ignatius somehow still finished second on PEDs. Goddamn slouch of an animal."

Jay withdrew $10,000 on September 27. The odds on an Ignatius win must've been long enough to turn the money into at least what was needed to pay for the procedure. Jay lost, yet by October 2 still somehow deposited $25,000 into his savings account, bringing it above the target $30,000 mark.

"Did he win on a second race a few days after?" Cole asks.

"He just did that one bet. After that shot to the wallet, I can't blame him."

Yet Jay still came up with $25,000. If cash that fast didn't come from gambling or a bank, it must've come from somewhere darker.

"Did he mention borrowing a chunk of money off the street?" Cole asks.

"I let him down with Ignatius. I've been embarrassed, avoided him the last couple weeks. I wouldn't know. Wish I could help. Sorry."

Cole nods. He shakes Flippy's hand and steps out of the Dodge.

"Hey bro," Flippy says. "You seem like you'd be a good

wingman. We should hit the town and crush some serious ass. Saturday night?"

"Saturday nights I have pottery class," Cole kids. "Thanks for the invite, though."

He unblocks the parking lot exit with his Jeep. But doesn't leave yet. He walks to the last hole on the mini-golf course.

Though faint, his mom's lines marking his height are still on the tree. At twelve, if he only knew he'd have just a couple more years with her, he never would've stopped their tradition here. He'd give up a lot to spend just one more birthday with her. He kisses two of his fingers, touches them to the bark, and heads back to his Jeep.

9

With a bucket of fried chicken under his arm, Cole walks down a dirt road. He got it at Zeek's, a favorite among locals. The aroma reminds him of autumn Friday nights in high school. After football games, if Timber Ridge won, he and his teammates would go to the restaurant with their girlfriends. The chef/owner Zeek would have tables reserved for them out back. He'd bring out free food, sit with the teenagers, and tell stories about Timber Ridge from before they were born.

The woods around Cole thicken, the paved cross street disappearing behind the foliage. The dirt road leads to a clearing where four cinderblock-propped RVs are arranged in a square, at the center an aboveground hot tub with a red heart painted on the side. He's heard about this place since he was fifteen, but never went until now.

At the front trailer, he knocks on a door. It opens, revealing a girl about twenty in lingerie, a silk robe, and Ugg boots. She smells like cocoa butter.

"Hey cowboy," she says. "Got an appointment?"

"I'm looking for Char."

"She doesn't see clients." The girl rubs the lapel of his coat.

"But I sure do. A room is a hundred an hour. Plus tip, depending on how cozy we get. What you in the mood for?"

Cole hasn't been with a woman in a while. The last two years he spent undercover on sensitive overseas missions. Letting someone get close, even for a night, could've jeopardized his cover and the safety of him and his fellow operatives.

"I actually didn't come here for that," he says. "Tell Char it's Cole, if you don't mind."

She looks him up and down. "Too bad." She turns around and slinks out of view.

Soon he hears a familiar voice, "Do I smell Zeek's?"

Char, short for Charlotte, steps to the doorway. A gray business suit drapes her slender, five-foot-ten body. She graduated Timber Ridge High the same year as Cole, where she dated his buddy, an interior lineman. At Quinn's birthday party, a former classmate mentioned Char took this place over from her uncle.

"Smelling that, seeing you," she says, "brings me right back. Remember when Gemma asked Zeek to whip up his nuclear hot sauce, then dared Hal to chug it?"

"He didn't play right for three weeks."

She laughs. They hug. "I caught wind about your brother," she says, the exuberance leaving her expression.

"Hoping you could give me a hand with that." He passes her the bucket of chicken. "Consider this a bribe."

"Mmm. But I'm sorry. I barely know Jay. He never came here if that's what you're asking."

"The Hadaway factory, hundreds of male workers between twenty and fifty. I'm assuming at least a few of them found their way here every now and then, right?"

"After they closed, my business took a major hit. Still hasn't recovered. Why?"

"I want to talk to an ex-employee. Got a current address for any of those guys?"

She waves him inside, leading him into the kitchen area of the RV. "Let me ask the girls." She paces out the back door to another trailer while he sits in a cramped booth.

Ten minutes later she returns, pulls a pair of paper plates from a cabinet, and tops each with a couple pieces of chicken. She sits across from him and bites her drumstick.

"Becky used to do house calls for a guy named Gary," Char says. "He hasn't come in since the layoffs. Prairie Street. She doesn't remember the number, but said the mailbox had some carving of an animal on it."

Cole bites into his wing. They catch up and he leaves for Prairie Street.

The middle-class neighborhood is similar to Cole's, nice yet unassuming homes on a couple acres apiece. He pulls up to one with a wooden buffalo atop the mailbox post. Cole wonders if this guy Gary, out of a job for over a year, could no longer afford a decent place like this and moved.

Cole rings the bell. No answer. Yet a Ford pickup is parked in the driveway. Cole peeks through a front window. Unlike the outside of the house, the inside is in disarray. Dirty dishes are piled in the kitchen sink, empty booze bottles on the den's floor, a hole in a wall. SportsCenter plays on the TV. Someone seems to be home.

Cole knocks on the window. He puts his ear to the glass. For a few seconds, he hears nothing besides the muffled banter of ESPN reporters. Then footsteps.

A man surfaces on the other side of the glass. His pudgy torso bulges under his mustard-stained tee shirt. His long, graying hair dangles over his reddish complexion.

"Get the hell off my property," he says. His voice slurs like he's drunk.

"Are you Gary?"

"The next payment for my truck is in the mail. Try to repossess it and I'll run your ass over."

"I'm not here to take anything from you, man." Cole pulls a fifty-dollar bill from his wallet. "All I want in return is a minute of your time."

Gary peers at the money for a moment longer, then disappears. The front door opens. Cole walks to it, pleased his money offer worked.

Then he realizes it didn't. A shotgun barrel juts out the doorway.

Gary cocks the weapon. "I'm not falling for any more tricks from you people. Get the fuck off my land now."

Cole raises his hands. "That's a nice Benelli. I've fired one a time or two. They're pretty loud." He nods at the neighbor's house. "If you blow me away, whoever lives there is going to hear the blast."

"Oh well."

"The cops will show up, search my body, see I was unarmed. When they run my driver's license, they'll see I wasn't a repo man or anyone else who was a danger to you. Sure, you could make up a story about how I tried to attack you. And maybe the court would buy it. But that would require a good defense attorney. Last I heard, they charge about five bills an hour. Kill me if you want. I just want to make sure you know what you're signing up for."

Gary's gaze jumps between the neighbor's house and Cole. He clutches the shotgun barrel with both hands, lunges out the doorway, and swings the butt at Cole's head.

Cole bends backward, the rifle cutting the air inches above him. It slams into Gary's shoulder. Cole clasps the butt and yanks the gun out of Gary's grip.

"Christ," Gary says, backpedaling toward the doorway. He seems both impressed and frightened. He tries to close the door, but Cole stops it with the rifle barrel.

Cole moseys into the house. He pockets the wallet, phone, and keys from the kitchen counter. Two full Jim Beam bottles and a halfway-done Absolut one stand atop the refrigerator. Cole uncaps the vodka bottle. He dumps it into the sink.

"What the fuck?" Gary says.

"I'm going to keep pouring out your supply until you talk to me." The last of the vodka vanishes down the drain.

"Talk about what?"

"After everyone at Hadaway lost their jobs, did anyone approach you guys about short-term money help, cash loans?"

Gary fidgets with the bottom of his shirt. "I'd rather not get into this, dude."

Cole grabs a Jim Beam bottle.

"Fine," Gary shouts.

"Who was it?"

"Wasn't one guy. A group. Bikers. Please don't tell them I was yapping about them. They sound like bad news."

"Any of your pals accept a loan?"

"Just one that I know of."

"What were the terms?"

"I don't know the specifics. He just said he had a bad experience, warned the rest of us to stay away."

Predatory lending. Gangs offer cash to disadvantaged people without the credit to go to a bank, at an interest rate similar to a bank's. Right after the money is accepted, the gangs renege on the promised rate, jack it higher, and threaten the borrower until paid.

Cole calls Char.

"You find him all right?" she asks.

"He mentioned bikers who may be into some nasty stuff. You ever hear of a local crew like this or is he giving me the runaround?"

"We had a couple guys pull up here on Harleys a few weeks ago. High on something, disrespecting the girls. I told them to leave. One grabbed me by the throat and pinned me against the wall. I thought he was going to strangle me. His friend said something like, she's just a skank, not worth it, and they left. Must be the same men. Freedom Riders. That's what it said on the back of their vests."

"You know where I could find these Freedom Riders?"

"If you somehow think they put Jay in his coma, I get how much you'd want revenge. But parts of Timber Ridge changed when you were away. These bikers are nothing like the people we grew up with. Or the engineers you were around on that oil rig. Sounds like Jay was out of his element. A sweet guy like you would be too. Please stay away."

"All I want to do is confirm if they were responsible. I'm not going to try to fight them."

"If you did, they'd murder you." She huffs. "I've recently been seeing a lot of Harleys parked outside the Knotted Vine when I pass by at night. You're just going to talk to them, right?"

"That's it. Thanks Char. So long."

He ends the call and glances at Gary. Cole removes the confiscated items from his pockets and sets them back on the counter. He empties the shotgun shells onto the floor and hands Gary the weapon.

Cole feels bad for him because of the layoffs, so gives him the fifty-dollar bill too, then puts on his aviator sunglasses and leaves.

10

Cole stands by the window in his den, considering his move against the Freedom Riders. The potbelly fireplace casts warmth through the one-story cabin. On the wall beside it is a tribal design, a wooden circle with hanging feathers. He sips a can of club soda, watching the sun descend behind a mountaintop. After nightfall he'll approach the bikers. In the meantime, he can make good on a promise.

He finds his neighbor Lacey Carter on Instagram and sends her a direct message:

Hey Lacey. I can build Declan's ramp today FYI. Cool if I stop by?

She responds:

Bring your appetite. I'm making pasta. Come around 6 if good.

He scrolls through her Instagram photos. He smiles at a shot of her at Adventure Park with Declan and his friends, the boys with paintball rifles, she in the middle forming a gun with her fingers like a Charlie's Angel. She seems like a good mom. And Declan a good son. Cole's favorite picture is one of the boy clenching his teeth carrying a bag of sod. Lacey captioned it *Man of the house helping mom in the garden.*

At six, Cole heads next door with a shovel and bottle of wine. Declan, on his bike, waves.

Cole makes a ramp while the boy observes. The angle is just steep enough where he can get some air, yet low enough where he can't hurt himself. Cole gives him some pointers and watches him go off a few times.

"Killin' it," Cole says. "You're a natural."

He fist-bumps Declan and walks inside to a delicious tomato-sauce scent.

Stirring a pot of linguini, Lacey peeks over her shoulder at him. She looks great in a fitted sweater and jeans. "Did he break his leg yet?" she asks with a smile.

"Just a toe."

Her expression stiffens.

He sticks out his tongue, then hands her the bottle of Pinot noir.

She chuckles. "You were about to make me drink this whole thing. Thank you. Want a glass?"

He gives her a thumbs-up. While she opens the bottle, he checks out her homemade Halloween decorations, a carved pumpkin on the counter, a white-bedsheet ghost in the corner, taped to the wall pieces of painted-black cardboard cut in the shape of bats. His attention moves to Declan out the window.

She passes Cole a glass of wine and says, "He talks about you a lot. He asked me to find a clip of one of your old football games on YouTube."

"Any luck?"

"Think you were before YouTube's time. No offense."

"Maybe better that way. These kids now, everything they do is documented on the internet. Got to be tough on them."

"On the parents too. I'm in constant fear Declan is going to make some adolescent mistake that follows him around the rest of his life."

"He has a level head for a boy his age. He won't cross any lines. I can tell."

"Good to hear." She mixes the pasta with the sauce. "I don't have any brothers. The thought of raising a boy was scary. Especially...after his dad decided not to stick around. To prepare myself, when I was pregnant, I went to Walmart and bought DVDs of all these dude movies. I'd be up at night intently watching them, making mental notes."

"Hysterical."

"Not sure how much it worked. But hey, at least I can do a really good Will Ferrell impersonation now." Mimicking his character from *Old School*, she says, "Bring your green hat."

Cole claps. "Yep."

She opens the window and calls out to Declan, "Ready."

Soon all three sit at the kitchen table, eating. The meal is as good as it looks. Declan gets up from the table and grabs a Polaroid camera from the den. He hands it to his mom and says, "Get one of me and Cole."

She says to Cole, "The kids use these ironically now. Remember when we used them because they were actually cool?"

He laughs. Declan stands beside him, flexing his triceps while pretending to appear natural. Lacey snaps the shot and the picture emerges.

While she shakes it, Declan picks up the camera and says, "Now let me get one of you two."

"You just took one of Cole," she says. "Let him finish his dinner."

Cole shrugs as if to say he's cool with it. Lacey shrugs too, then smiles for the camera.

"You guys are like a mile apart," Declan says. "Get closer."

She blushes. Then nudges her chair a few inches closer to Cole's.

"Come on, Ma," Declan says. "Little more." She moves a few inches nearer, blushing more. He takes the picture and grins when the image clarifies. He hands it to Cole. "You keep it. Souvenir from the Carter house."

Once dinner is done, Declan goes into the next room to watch TV.

Lacey says to Cole, "I can open another bottle of wine if you're up for it."

Though he would love to have a second bottle with her, he needs to stay sharp for his move against the Freedom Riders later.

He checks the time on his phone. "Thanks for having me. But I've got to go over a bunch of blueprints tonight for a construction project."

"Do your thing. This was fun."

"It was." They hug. He points at Declan in the next room and, loud enough for him to hear, says, "Your son is a beast on a bike, by the way."

Declan smiles. He and Cole wave bye to each other.

Back at his cabin, Cole sets the Polaroid on the bookshelf in his den. He and Lacey look good next to each other. The kid might be on to something.

Cole works on his canoe for a while, then drives to The Knotted Vine bar.

11

Heavy metal music booms out of a log building labeled *The Knotted Vine*. It sits on five or so acres, nothing around but trees touched with the rural, eleven-PM darkness. Cole marches past the row of Harley Davidsons parked out front. He thinks about one of the many Native American lessons Powaw and his wife, now deceased from cancer, passed down to him and Jay.

The Native American couple was unable to have natural offspring. They adopted the Maddox brothers as teenagers after their biological mother and father died in a car accident caused by an overturned logging truck. A key teaching of Powaw and his wife was never continuing a relationship with someone who uses you.

His last few years in the military, Cole sensed the decisions of high-ranking US Army officials were based more on partisan politics than the interests of American citizens. Though this bothered him, he stuck to his job and completed his operations.

That changed after his Feng Liao mission in Greece.

After going through Feng's phone, Cole learned Feng was not planning an attack on the US power grid. He was planning to expose how one of the largest tech companies in America stole sensitive personal data from hundreds of millions of users.

The company's CEO happens to be one of the President's biggest donors. Government insiders wanted Feng silenced. And Cole was tricked into executing an innocent man with three children. Cole was used. He had no option but to leave the army.

These bikers tried to use Jay with a sham interest rate. Jay had no option but to object. And they smashed in his skull for it.

Cole steps into The Knotted Vine, neon beer-logo signs burning against the shadows. A male singer with a face of piercings screams into a microphone, similar-looking guys on the guitar and drums.

Cole's visited this place a few times over the years on break. He remembers a classic rock band. And patrons in tucked-in flannel shirts and cowboy hats, Hadaway workers and ranch hands. The customers tonight wear a lot of dark colors, many with skinheads.

Saloon-style doors lead to a rear room where men eat and drink in black-leather vests. On the backs are *Freedom Riders*, skulls in American flag bandanas, and *Montana*.

"Easy fella, can't go in there," the bartender says. "Reserved seating."

"I'll only be a sec," Cole says.

He enters the windowless, red-walled room, the table covered in plates of food and pitchers of beer. Five bikers sit with three attractive, tattooed girls in crop tops. Everyone peers at the intruder.

Cole recognizes the men's faces from social media research he did earlier on the Freedom Riders.

"Sorry for interrupting," he says. "My brother told me he knows you guys. Jay Maddox."

Silence. The smoke from a cigar wafts around the table.

"I'm here to cover his debt," Cole says. He removes a checkbook and pen from his back pocket. "Tell me how much he owes."

His gaze sweeps the men's faces. None responds, but a couple whisper to each other.

The guy at the head of the table stands. Mid-forties, sand-colored handlebar moustache, a broad trunk and meaty, potent arms. He must be the leader. "We don't know anyone by that name."

Accepting a check to repay a debt would establish a paper trail, proof in court the bikers loaned money to a victim of a savage beating. Cole is now confident the Freedom Riders are responsible. If so, additional evidence should be out there that the gang can't avoid in court. He will urge the police to investigate them to find it.

"Understood," Cole says, slipping the checkbook and pen back in his pocket.

"Who do you think you are barging in here on me and my friends?" the biker asks.

"I'm not anyone."

"You a cop?"

"I'm just a safety inspector. I don't want any trouble." Cole turns and steps in the direction of the saloon doors.

"Hold up."

Cole stops.

The biker struts around the table. "If your brother John told you he borrowed money from a group of bikers, it wasn't us. So don't go around saying that, giving the wrong impression to people."

John. Nice touch.

"Jay," Cole says.

The biker smirks. "I get the feeling this other group of bikers gave your brother Jay some grief for not paying back his debt. I got that right?"

"Put him in a coma."

"Let me give you some advice for him. If he wakes up from this coma, he shouldn't go tattling on whoever roughed him up. See, if he did, this other motorcycle club may make things even worse for him." He nods at Cole. "They might come after family members. Like a brother. Maybe a wife. Maybe even a kid."

Cole has been around plenty of men like this. They prey upon weakness. Now that this guy threatened Melanie and Quinn, Cole can't remain neutral.

"I think you're lying to me," Cole says. "I think you know exactly what happened to my brother. Now let me give you some advice. Don't talk about my family anymore."

The biker snickers. "If I put a new bathroom in my house, I'll give you a call to inspect the shitter. Until then, get the fuck out of my face." He grasps Cole's shoulder and tries to turn him toward the exit.

Cole clasps his hand, twists it into an outside wrist lock, and shoves him. The biker staggers backward. He slams into the table, knocking off a pitcher of beer and a couple plates.

Cole bent his wrist hard enough to apply painful strain on the ulnocarpal joint, yet not enough to break a bone. If the biker scurried out of the back room for the hospital, the bartender could've noticed and called the cops.

The biker's cheeks redden with embarrassment. He stands, gropes about the table, and grabs a steak knife.

"Slice him up, Russell," a Freedom Rider with a hoop earring says. He's much younger than the rest, early twenties.

Russell creeps toward Cole with the blade in front of him.

"I'll give you three chances to stab me with that," Cole says. Then puts his hands behind his back. "I'll even keep these here for you."

Russell's grip tightens on the steak knife, white spots on his knuckles.

He swipes the blade at Cole's face.

Cole whips his head to the side, out of the way. "That's one."

Russell grunts. He bends his knees in an athletic stance. And circles Cole to the right. He lunges forward, thrusting the knife at his stomach.

Cole twists his hips, evading it. "Two."

Russell's eyes flick to the table as if to gauge the reaction of his troops. Cole steps backward, stands just in front of the puddle of spilt beer. Russell rocks side to side, as if trying to get Cole off balance. Cole stands still.

Russell swings at him with his left fist. Cole ducks the punch. Russell's right hand comes down at his head with the knife. Cole hops backward, eluding it, landing on the other side of the puddle. Russell's front foot meets it. He slips and goes down hard.

The beer on the floor soaks his jeans. His men look away.

"That was your third chance," Cole says. He moves his hands from his back to his sides. "Try it again and I'm going to do a lot more with that blade than dodge it."

Russell's pale-blue eyes blink a couple times. He stays down.

Cole strides through the saloon doors.

12

Cole clenches the wheel of his Jeep, his breathing heavy. He's parked in the woods across the street from The Knotted Vine, his lights and engine off. After Russell's threat on the Maddox family, everything changed.

If the Freedom Riders are willing to hurt innocent Melanie and Quinn, they are even more dangerous than Cole expected. The underfunded local police, used to investigating public urination and the occasional mugging, are no match for a cold-blooded, organized-crime adversary.

Cole will have to go after them himself. Not just Jay's attacker, but the entire crew.

For all their negatives, gangs tend to be loyal. If Jay wakes up and testifies against his assailant, fellow bikers may retaliate against Melanie and Quinn. Cole counted eleven Freedom Riders total from his social media research. With a singular, powerful strike, he needs to put all eleven in prison, where they can do no harm.

He sits in the darkness among the hoots of owls for over two hours till the bar closes, his shearling coat providing some defense against the cold. A leather-vested guy exits and strides to the Harleys. More trickle out behind him. A minute later Russell emerges with a bleach-blond girl.

He stumbles on the way to his bike as if intoxicated. The girl tries to help him but he brushes her hand away. He mounts his motorcycle and fumbles with his keys. She watches him, her silver-studded purse glistening under a light. He grabs her wrist and tugs her to him. She climbs on the seat behind him.

Engines rev. One biker goes east. Russell takes off west, three others following.

Cole starts his Jeep and turns in that direction. He hangs back on the road, just close enough to keep them in view.

Russell makes a right, one of the other Freedom Riders continuing straight, the other two trailing the leader. Cole eases off the gas, dropping another fifty feet or so behind them.

The trio of remaining bikes and Jeep wind a road up the mountain, no more buildings around, just big trees and black sky. A man turns, now just one bike between Cole and Russell.

The vehicles continue up the road for about two miles, reaching a stop sign. Russell hooks a left, splitting off from the other biker, and disappears on the other side of the woods.

Cole debates speeding up, but opts against it. Russell could make him.

Cole brakes at the next intersection. Nothing in the area is open this late. So Russell is heading home. If he lived outside Timber Ridge, he wouldn't be this far up the mountain, instead would've veered toward the county highway lower.

Left of the stop sign, Coneflower Road extends to meet three residential streets before sloping farther upward to the wealthy part of town, where people like real estate developer Wayne Shaw live. Even if Russell generates enough illegal income to afford a mansion up there, a flaunting purchase like that could provoke the IRS. His house must be on one of the three streets that intersects Coneflower before its big incline.

Cole cruises to the first, idles, looks for a Harley in a driveway. Nothing. He drives to the second block. No motorcycles. The third, none either. It must be in a garage.

Cole parks at the edge of the woods and skulks through the shadows to the first house on the street. He opens its mailbox. Nothing inside. He sneaks to the next house, checks the box, a couple catalogues, the first name on them *Veronica*.

He continues this routine for all the homes on the street. With no luck. He moves to the next block, repeats the process. No success at the first seven houses.

But at the eighth, a power bill addressed to a *Russell Garnold*. Cole makes a mental note of the address, *627 Sovard Court*.

An upstairs light bleeds through a curtain. Cole slinks to the fenced backyard. On the deck is a chrome dog-food bowl labeled *Lucifer*, beside it a bone with deep gnaw marks.

Cole's collected enough intel to move to the next leg of his strategy. Now he needs supplies.

13

The sun rises, streaks of yellow over the mountaintops. Cole lies on a hill in the woods overlooking Russell's property. He watches the home through binoculars, a formfitting balaclava hat covering his face.

In his backpack are more supplies. One required a two-and-a-half-hour trip yesterday to a specialty electronics store in Helena.

No activity at Russell's so far. Then one of the garage doors opens, unveiling his Harley with him on it. The bleach-blonde from The Knotted Vine hugs him from the backseat. The bike pulls out of the driveway, the garage door closing behind.

Cole waits for it to cruise to the end of Sovard Court and turn. He descends the hill through thick brush.

At Russell's garage, he pulls a straightened coat hanger from his backpack. He maneuvers the hooked end between the top of a garage door and its frame and jimmies it around until he feels it meet the door-release cable. He yanks it. The door now free, he pushes it up on its tracks with his leather-gloved hands, slips inside, and closes it behind him.

The dog in the house starts barking.

Cole folds up the hanger tool, puts it in his bag, and removes a Saran Wrapped sausage he cooked this morning.

He whistles. "You hungry, Lucifer?"

He holds the sausage to the bottom of the door, feeding the scent into the house, then opens the door and chucks the link over his shoulder.

A Rottweiler about a hundred fifty pounds barrels toward the sausage. Munching on it, Lucifer sees Cole. The dog charges at him. Cole lunges inside and slams the door. It quivers as Lucifer's big paws punch at it.

Among loud barking, Cole walks a short hallway into the kitchen and turns into the foyer. The house has an odd odor, like stale bread. He assesses the few items in the room, a coatrack, a mirror, a mounted display of half a dozen photos, one of a man in a Vietnam-era helmet and fatigues.

From a zipped compartment of his bag, Cole pulls out a circular black object about the diameter of a quarter and peels a clear plastic coating off its underside. He sticks the small object to the bottom of the mirror frame.

A motorcycle engine rumbles outside. Cole did not anticipate Russell's return this early. Not even ten minutes have passed. If Russell notices his dog trapped in the garage, he'll realize something is wrong.

Cole darts through the kitchen toward the hallway door. At this angle, he spots a silver-studded purse on the counter. Russell's girlfriend must've forgotten it.

Cole opens the door to the garage. Lucifer hurtles into the house. While Cole closes the door, the dog tries to bite his calf. He deflects the fangs with the bag.

He backpedals into the kitchen. The dog tries to bite his ankle. Cole's arms extend downward to block it, the fabric of his sweatshirt sleeve nudging up a bit.

Lucifer leaps, trying to chomp his crotch. Cole prevents that, but a tooth penetrates the exposed flesh of his lower forearm. It draws blood, a red drop hitting the white-tile floor.

The garage drones open.

Cole kneels on the blood, dabbing it from sight with his jeans, then hurries into the bathroom and shuts the door. He lowers his sleeve over his cut.

The tap of high heels is audible between barks. A feminine voice says, "What you mad about, Loo?"

Lucifer's barking nears, just on the other side of the bathroom door, as if alerting her about a problem inside.

The barking doesn't let up. The doorknob turns.

Cole places his backpack between his legs and presses his back to the wall. He fans his feet outward. The door opens. It moves toward his nose. He turns his head, the door stopping less than an inch from him.

The woman's blond hair appears in the sliver of space beneath the top hinge. Cole holds his breath.

She peeks inside the shadowy bathroom. A few seconds go by.

"Everything's okay, Loo," she says.

Her head goes away. But she doesn't shut the door. Cole's knees and ankles hurt keeping his feet fanned.

"Gimme a kiss," she says.

Cole hears the jangle of purse buckles and more high-heeled footsteps. She's leaving. But before she's gone, the dog runs into the bathroom.

Cole grabs the top of the door and tucks his legs to his stomach, careful to keep his noise to a minimum.

Lucifer stands on its hind legs. Its teeth latch onto the heel of Cole's boot. Its paws push against the door, closing it. Cole's fingers are squashed between it and the frame. Pain pulsates through them.

He struggles to hold back a groan. He listens to the woman's steps. The house door closes. Then the garage. The motorcycle bellows, then the sound softens as it distances down the block.

But Cole is not done. He needs to exit the house without an identifying trace. No more bloody dog bites.

He shakes his boot from Lucifer's mouth, jumps down from the door, and grabs the bathroom's metal wastebasket.

The dog scrambles to him. Cole slides the receptacle over its hulking head, a couple tissues falling out. Lucifer thrashes. The spikes on its collar clatter against the metal.

Cole grasps his bag and backs into the kitchen. Lucifer escapes the wastebasket. Cole re-contains its head before being bitten, careful not to hurt the animal, just control it.

He opens the door to the garage a bit, squeezes through, and shoves it closed. On the other side, he hears the receptacle fall off Lucifer's head.

When Russell comes home, Cole hopes he'll believe the dog was just playing with the wastebasket, not battling a former black-ops commando with an agenda.

Cole pockets a morsel of sausage still in the garage, closes it, and veers to the front of the house. He removes a white envelope from his bag. *Russell* is written on it in black marker. Cole slips it under the front door into the foyer, then jogs to his Jeep up in the woods.

The envelope is intended to work in conjunction with the object Cole stuck to the mirror in the foyer, a spy bug. He just set the type of trap he once used on a terrorist leader in Somalia. It won't be the singular knock-out blow Cole needs, but can point him in the right direction.

14

Cole sits on the couch in his den, reading a crease-cornered paperback titled *Wisdom of the Clear Moon*. A high school graduation gift from Powaw and his late wife, it's filled with pithy insights from Native American culture.

Cole had it with him overseas, the cover faded from much exposure to the Middle Eastern sun. He's read the seventeen-year-old book multiple times, the same insights seeming to grow in meaning at different stages of his life.

He flips to a new page:

What we may search for far and wide can often be found by our side.

While he reads, he listens to an audio broadcast from his new burner phone, resting on the sofa arm. The small black bug on the bottom of Russell's mirror transmits a live feed of his foyer.

Over the last seven hours, Cole's heard no noise of interest. Then he makes out a grumble like the sound of an opening garage door.

He sets down the book. In a bit, he hears Russell say, "Hey Loo. How's the big guy? What you doing with the garbage?"

The dog lets out fast barks as if trying to tell him about the uninvited visitor before. Cole hears nothing else for about half a minute.

Then Russell says, "What the hell?" His voice comes through louder than before. He must be closer to the bug, in the foyer. And he must've just opened the *Russell* envelope.

Cole left a note for him inside:

The feds know what you guys are up to. Be careful.

Soon Russell says, "Yo. I just walked in on some real weird shit...Some note under my door about the feds being on to us. Unsigned...Says be careful at the end, like it's from a friend...But maybe it's a threat...Could be that Maddox asshole from The Knotted Vine trying to get in my head...Jesus Christ, Dugan, I already told you I don't know...To play it safe, let's clean the drugs out of the—"

A bark from Lucifer, Cole unable to hear the last thing Russell said.

"We should do it after all the other stores in the area are closed too, nine o'clock," Russell says. "Get the word out. Whoever you send, make sure they watch their asses, be ready to throw down if they got to...Yeah, bye."

Cole's tactic worked, but not in full. As he hoped, his note about *The feds* prompted Russell to call a gang lieutenant and discuss on tape a federal crime the Freedom Riders are involved in. They are trafficking drugs. If Cole can uncover hard proof, he'd put them away for a long time. But he missed a key detail during that dog bark. He doesn't know where they're hiding their stash.

On the bug, Russell said "other stores." The gang seems to be stashing their narcotics at a local business. Russell doesn't want anyone nearby to see them move the supply tonight at nine. Cole would think the store is on Main Street, the only section of

Timber Ridge where shops are close enough for anyone to scope what's going on next door.

He rules out anything in the vicinity of Gold Sparrow or the movie theater since they're both open past nine, till eleven.

On his new phone, he pulls up a street-view map of Main and scrolls past storefronts away from the diner and theater.

He looks up the hours of Bradford Outfitters. It's open till seven, but everything around closes by six. Same with the pet store and nail salon.

Next he scrolls to Harris Meats. Powaw was friends with old Mister Harris who ran the place. They'd go to the rodeo together. Around a year ago, Powaw mentioned he passed away. His widow could've sold the business.

It closes at eight. Cole checks the hours of the stores in sight. The latest-open one closes at nine.

In addition to its centralized location for distributing drugs through Timber Ridge, Harris Meats would make for an effective money-laundering front for the gang's illicit profits. It's an established brand that yields solid, consistent revenue, plenty of it cash.

It seems to be the winner. But Cole still wants further evidence.

Before he leaves the house to get it, he Googles "narcotics Timber Ridge MT." Scanning news articles, he learns the American opioid epidemic infested his hometown right around the time of the Hadaway closure.

A dozen fentanyl-related fatalities just last year, in a place with only a few thousand residents. All twelve deaths were deemed accidental, no suicides. The Freedom Riders could be selling counterfeit prescription pills, laced in secret with lethal fentanyl. The potent substance lets manufacturers churn out more drugs for less money, raising profits.

Obituaries come up for the victims. Three of them were minors, one seventeen, another sixteen, another just thirteen. Cole recognizes a kid's last name, Igelsey, and sees he was a nephew of an old friend, a football teammate back in high school.

Cole lets out a long exhale, then grabs his coat.

15

Cole exits Home Depot with a bag of lockpick tools and black spray paint. Earlier, he went to the chamber of commerce and found the record for Harris Meats. It's no longer owned by the Harris family, but a holding company with the vague name TR Foods. Which happens to be based in Panama, a preferred location for shell corporations cleaning cash.

His operating window between eight and nine PM at Harris's should be enough time to confiscate any stashed narcotics, but only if nothing goes wrong.

He eats dinner in town and heads back to his cabin. A bit of a draft comes from the den.

On his shut-off TV's blackened screen is a reflection of a shattered window.

Heavy footsteps approach him.

A broad-shouldered man in a hoodie stomps to Cole with a 9mm pistol in his hand. Cole recalls him from the back room of The Knotted Vine. A biker in his forties with an L-shaped facial scar. The gun rises toward Cole's head.

Cole kicks him in the chest. The biker stumbles into the wall. The bookshelf rattles, the Polaroid of Cole and Lacey falling off.

The biker attempts to re-aim the gun, but Cole grabs his wrist, angling the barrel to the ceiling.

The biker knees him in the stomach, knocking the wind out of him, and yanks his gun hand free. He points the 9mm at Cole, who rolls through the doorway into the kitchen and scrambles behind the wall.

Pluchoo. A bullet whizzes into the kitchen, exploding a coffee canister on the counter island.

Cole crawls to the side of the island opposite the doorway.

Pluchoo. The biker fires at the cabinetry under the countertop, but the cast-iron pots and pans inside stop the bullet from hitting Cole.

The biker approaches from the right, his motorcycle boots clunking on the hardwood. Cole slips off his own boots to soften his footfalls, then darts left to the refrigerator and opens it.

Pluchoo, a round nails the stainless-steel door, Cole behind it for protection. He reaches into the fridge, grabs a can of club soda, and shakes it, the carbonation hardening it. He hurls it at the biker.

It drills his head. He lurches against the sink. His eyelids flutter. He's fazed. Before he can re-aim the gun, Cole chucks a second can at it. The weapon is knocked from the biker's grip. It clatters through the doorway back into the den.

The biker shuffles after it. Cole runs at him. And tackles him before he gets it.

The men slam onto the coffee table, shattering the glass. The biker elbows Cole in the abdomen, then stands and delivers a knee toward his face.

Cole avoids it, clasps the biker's foot, and rips it inward, tearing his peroneus longus tendon. The biker's face crashes down to the jagged glass on the area rug. He groans turning over.

Cole mounts him and decks his nose. Cole feels it break, then punches him again.

Blood pours from the biker's nostrils. "Enough, man. You win."

Cole climbs off him, picks up the loose gun, and secures it in the rear waist of his jeans. "Was coming here really worth all this pain?"

"When I was locked up, every week like clockwork, Russell would have a paper bag of cash delivered to my old lady. No questions asked. He was loyal to me. And I'm loyal to him. What you did to him at the bar, that shit just wasn't right. You slip that envelope under his door too?"

"Tell Russell to stock up on paper bags. I'm turning you in to the police." Cole fishes his phone from his pocket.

The biker unsheathes a knife from his boot.

He rises to his knees and stabs it at Cole's stomach.

Cole turns out of its path, grabs the biker's hand, and reverses the direction of the blade. He leans his weight on it, driving it into the biker's chest.

The man gasps. He coughs, a splash of blood in his mouth. His eyes go big, then small. His arms flop to his sides.

Cole peers down at the still guy bleeding all over his rug and scratches his forehead. A dead body will complicate things.

He checks the time on his phone, 7:37 PM, just twenty-three minutes till the butcher shop closes. Also on his screen is a text from Lacey: *Was that gunshots we just heard at your house?*

He replies: *Heard that too. The woods behind my place. Must be hunters out late.*

His neighbor on the other side, a reclusive old woman, might've heard the shots too. She could've called the cops.

Who could be on their way.

16

His boots back on, Cole dashes to the wall of his garage where he keeps supplies for work. He slips on a pair of construction gloves, grabs two bungee cords, and runs past the mess of shattered glass and blood in his den into his kitchen. If his reclusive neighbor called the cops, he has no more than ten minutes to clear the scene.

Yes, the killing was in self-defense, but he'd still be hauled down to the station, forced to stay for hours answering questions, maybe even spend the night in a cell until a lawyer arrives. Tonight's plan at the butcher shop would be ruined, plus a manslaughter charge could hit him if authorities don't believe his story.

From the cabinet beneath the kitchen sink, he snatches a Hefty box, then pulls the biker's motorcycle keys from his pocket and tosses them in a trash bag. He takes out his wallet and scopes the driver's license. Earl Laughlin, forty-one.

Cole chucks the wallet in the bag, collects Earl's phone from his pants, and taps the screen. Locked. He lifts Earl's dead thumb to it, the print unlocking it, then navigates to the settings and disables locking so he can get back in later. The phone goes in Cole's pocket.

He adds Earl's gun to the bag and rips the knife from his chest. Blood spills out onto the carpet and hardwood. He drops the blade in the bag, pulls another from the Hefty box, and slides it over Earl's head and torso. A bungee cord is wrapped around it beneath the stab wound, sealing off blood flow.

He kicks his coffee table off the area rug, rolls Earl up in it, and fastens it with the other cord.

From his closet, Cole grabs a mop, Pine-Sol, and a bucket. He fills it with sink water and rushes to clean the blood off his hardwood.

With his ticking-away time constraint, he can't pick up all the broken glass by the table and window, but hand-collects the bigger shards and drops them in the kitchen garbage pail.

The cleaning supplies go back in the closet. He glances outside the garage to make sure nobody is watching, unlocks his Jeep in the driveway, and crams into the trunk the rug-wrapped corpse and Earl's belongings. He stuffs his blood-streaked gloves and shearling coat in the trash bag and loads a few more items in the Jeep.

It rolls out of his driveway. The daylight is almost gone. *7:45 PM* on the console clock. The Freedom Riders will whisk away the drugs by nine. Before then, Cole needs to dispose of a body and break into the butcher shop.

No motorcycle in sight. To avoid suspicion, Earl must've parked a bit away from the cabin and walked. Cole would like to find the bike and move it out of the area but doesn't have time.

He travels a two-lane road with a gradual slope upward, entering a quiet section of town, no businesses around but the empty Hadaway factory.

He coasts to a stop in a clearing at Banshee Point, a rugged area of wilderness bordering Jackrabbit Canyon Lake, heaves the corpse over his shoulder, and lugs it down a steep hill of aspen trees to the lake.

After a trip back to the Jeep, he drops a dumbbell from his garage's weight set in the bag of his and Earl's belongings and chucks it into the shadowy lake with a big splash. He inserts two twenty-pound weights and one ten in the rolled rug, then caps off each end with a Hefty bag, limiting air bubbles.

He kicks the body across the tall grass into the water, takes off his balaclava hat and leather gloves, and descends a dirt road away from Banshee Point. The sky is now black, *8:24 PM* on the Jeep's clock. He rides toward Harris Meats.

Accessing the stashed drugs in only thirty-six minutes will be difficult. But if he works fast, with no hitches, he maybe can do it.

Then a hitch. In his rearview mirror, the blues and reds of police lights spin against the night.

17

The cop emerges from his vehicle. The short one with the bowl cut from Jay's crime scene, Hannelson.

Cole rolls down the window, smiling. "Evening, Officer."

Hannelson eyes Cole through his thick glasses. "You injured, Mister Maddox?"

"I'm fine. Why?"

"The business that went on. At your house."

Cole pretends to be perplexed. "I haven't been home in a while. I've been working late. What happened at my house?"

"We got a disturbing call from your neighbor Mrs. Sowapple. Said she heard gunshots coming from your cabin. Said she'd been living in her house for the better part of a century and knew the sound of a hunting shot...which these were not. We sent a deputy over to check on you. He noticed a broken window. Sarge thought you could've been hurt, so put it over the radio for us to keep 'em peeled for your Jeep."

"That's...scary."

"I was just on radar duty and spotted you pass. Sarge will have more info for you. I'll get her over the walkie. Sit tight."

"I'll just give her a call when I get home."

"She'll want to talk to you tonight." He pulls a walkie-talkie off his belt and speaks into it.

Cole glimpses the time.

Hannelson reattaches his walkie-talkie to his hip and says to Cole, "You're in pretty decent shape. I'm a bit of a sportsman myself."

"Cool."

"I'm into ultimate. You know…Frisbee."

"Sure."

"They've got a league down at the Y. Saturday mornings. I've been in it for years. You ought to come to a match for a look-see. Maybe it's something you'd want to sign up for. Great exercise. Let me tell you…a doozy for the quads."

Hannelson's gaze lingers near Cole's left armpit. Cole glances there, noticing a dab of Earl's blood about the size of a postage stamp on his white tee shirt.

Hannelson drifts away from the open window. He paces by his cruiser, out of Cole's earshot, talking on his radio.

Cole debates telling the truth, admitting to killing Earl in self-defense. But altering his story at this point could be worse. The cops could wonder why he first lied. They may discredit his self-defense claim and conclude he was covering up a murder.

The lights of a second squad car appear on the horizon. It cruises past them, U-turns, and parks behind the first.

Sergeant Sandra steps out, a black fleece vest over her uniform. She walks to Hannelson. They converse, both with grave expressions.

Keeping his eyes ahead and abdomen steady, Cole reaches his right arm to the backseat and feels around for the plastic Home Depot shopping bag. His fingertips meet the thin material. He slips his middle finger through a handle, drags the bag off the seat onto the car floor, and sticks his hand inside.

He pats the spray paint can. Then the lockpick kit. He opens it, feels around some more, and slips out an S-rake tool, metal with a pointy tip.

He slides it under his shirt, slices the flesh beneath his left armpit, deep enough to draw blood, and drops the tool in the space between his seat and the center console.

Sandra approaches the Jeep, a red-and-blue halo around her from the cop-car lights. She surveys Cole, her focus hovering over the blood mark. Hannelson must've told her about it. She lifts her eyes to his and asks, "Are you familiar with a man named Earl Laughlin?"

"Can't say I am."

"On the way back from your cabin, my deputy noticed a Harley Davidson parked behind the Nyacks' shed. No way old Lucille Nyack bought it for herself. Or would let her husband Al ride around on one. We ran the plate. Belongs to an Earl Laughlin. He's affiliated with a group called the Freedom Riders. Ever hear of them?"

"Sorry. What are they, like a motorcycle club?"

"Its members have lengthy criminal records. Earl Laughlin no exception. My theory is he burglarized your cabin tonight. Any idea why he would target your place?"

"Must've known I wasn't home."

"Right. Strange though, if you weren't there, not sure why he'd unload his firearm."

Cole acts disturbed. "What of mine did he shoot?"

"We're trying to find that out. Mind letting us in? We can have a look around, see what exactly he was up to. Check if anything of value is missing."

"Is it possible he's still there?"

"I doubt it. But we'll escort you just to be sure."

"I'm pretty drained. If you don't think he's there, I should get some sleep. Stop by for your search first thing tomorrow morning?"

She says nothing for a moment, her jaw undulating as she chews gum. "Timber Ridge is generally a pretty quiet town, wouldn't you say?"

He nods.

"First your brother is viciously assaulted," she says. "Then a few days later, we get an attempted robbery with a deadly weapon at your cabin. And find a motorcycle nearby that belongs to a member of a biker gang. Does all of that feel like a coincidence to you?"

He taps his fingers on the steering wheel. "It is definitely weird. You think this group, the Freedom Riders, you think they have it out for my family?"

"Not quite sure what's going on yet."

"I'm sure you guys will figure it out."

"Nice of you to trust us with that."

An eighteen-wheeler roars past them. She waits for the noise to die down, then points at the blood mark on his shirt. "What happened there, Mister Maddox?"

He looks at it. And pretends to spot it for the first time. "Hmm. I'm coming from a job repairing an oven. I must've caught myself on the edge of its door." He lifts his shirt, exposing the cut on his torso from the lockpick tool, establishing the blood is his, not soon-to-be-reported-missing Earl's.

She squints. "Whose oven were you repairing?"

"A woman's from Stoud Hollow. It was a side project my brother committed to. I'm trying to cover for him while he's laid up."

"That's awfully kind of you." Her eyes are still squinted. Despite his explanation of the blood, she still does not seem to believe his story. "Put some Neosporin on that cut. And get some rest. I'll be over at seven AM sharp tomorrow."

"See you then." He rolls up the window.

8:49 PM. He drives toward his cabin, then turns once out of view of the police cars, rerouting to the butcher shop. He won't have time for his original plan. He'll have to improvise.

18

Cole's Jeep zips into downtown Timber Ridge at 9:03 PM. Brick-facade businesses, all closed at this hour, line this stretch of Main Street, light from streetlamps reflecting on their shadowy windows. The sidewalks are empty.

He parks a block from the butcher shop, a faded illustration of a pig on its awning beside *Harris Meats*. No sign of anything suspect out front. He puts on his balaclava hat and leather gloves, slips his burner phone in his pocket, and grabs the Home Depot bag with the pick tools and can of paint.

He walks toward Harris's. His coat at the bottom of the lake, the wind chills his bare forearms.

A noise. An engine. Behind the store. He turns into the alley between it and an insurance shop. He kneels and inches his face to the corner.

Exhaust fumes spew from the tailpipe of an idling van, the Harris Meats logo on the side, the back double doors opened. Inside is a plastic crate the size of a large suitcase.

A burly, bearded guy lingers nearby, a Freedom Riders vest over a red Henley. Soon, a second large man in the bikers' vest, waxed-bald head, struts through the propped-open rear door of the shop with another plastic crate. He kicks the doorstop, the door closing, and loads the container into the van.

The bikers are preparing to leave. Cole needs to make a decision fast. He could follow the van to wherever it's going next, try to sneak in, and take the narcotics. But that option is rife with unknowns. If the Freedom Riders own Harris's, evidence of the drugs on their property would establish a direct link.

He'd planned to spray-paint Harris's security-camera lenses so the Freedom Riders couldn't see him and recognize him by his build. Based on his note to Russell, after the narcotics were gone, the bikers could've expected a raid by the feds versus Cole himself.

But that luxury is now gone.

Cole knots the top of the Home Depot bag and paces to the two bikers, his footsteps getting their attention.

"'Sup guys?" Cole says.

They stare at him. Cole remembers the bald one from The Knotted Vine. The guy maintains a hardened grimace, but the small muscles around an eye quiver.

The bearded one's hand creeps backward as if going for a weapon in the waist of his jeans.

"Don't do it," Cole says.

The biker's hand stops.

"One way or another, I'm gonna take what's in the van," Cole says. "I recommend you walk away and just let me do that. If you want to resist, I get it. But it won't work. And you'll end up hurt."

The Freedom Riders look at each other. The bald one nods.

The bearded one's hand rushes to his back, then rushes forward again, now in it a .45 pistol.

Gripping the Home Depot bag near the knot, Cole whips the metal spray-paint can and tools into the back of the biker's hand, crushing his capitate bone.

The gun falls from his grip. Cole kicks it under the van and kicks the outside of the guy's knee, caving it in. Cole spins his head backward to get eyes on the second biker. The man does not have a gun, yet is not weaponless, fastening brass knuckles over his fist.

The first biker throws a right hook. Cole blocks it with his forearm and headbutts him in the mouth. The guy topples to his back, blood oozing from his split lip. He struggles to stand on his hobbled leg.

While Cole pivots to the second biker, pain vibrates through his midsection. The brass knuckles just bashed his rib cage. The sixth rib on his right side feels cracked.

The metal fist speeds toward him for a second shot. But Cole leans to the side, dodging it. He grabs the biker's wrist and jerks him into the side of the van. His head clunks it.

Cole grasps the back of the woozy man's neck and slams his skull's frontal bone into a hubcap. The biker plops to the ground unconscious.

The first Freedom Rider, crawling under the van toward his gun, says into his phone, "Get your ass to the fucking butcher shop."

Grasping his ankle, Cole drags him out from under the van, then swings open the passenger door into his head, knocking him out.

Cole slips the pistol in his jeans, takes a couple seconds to catch his breath, and starts shooting a video of the butcher-shop property with his burner phone.

"I'm Cole Maddox," he says toward the microphone, "former member of the Seventy-Fifth Ranger Regiment of the US Army, and another unit I am not at liberty to speak of. This is a video for the Billings, Montana branch of the Drug Enforcement Administration. I am at Harris Meats in Timber Ridge, what I believe is now a money-laundering front controlled by a band of men who call themselves the Freedom Riders."

He points the camera at the out-cold bikers, recording the Freedom Riders insignia on the backs of their vests. At the van's rear, he lifts the lids of the two plastic crates, revealing stuffed-together clear bags of pills, tens of thousands.

"As you can see," he says, "they were attempting to transport what look to be oxycodone pills. Likely made with fentanyl. I'll be keeping my eyes on the supply until the DEA arrives in town to claim it." He ends the video.

He closes the van's rear doors, hops behind the wheel, and pulls onto the road.

A motorcycle engine growls behind him. Cole scopes the side-view mirror. A man in a leather vest flies toward him on a Harley.

He must be the backup the other Freedom Rider called.

Cole leans on the gas pedal, accelerating to sixty miles per hour. Then seventy. The growl behind him loudens. The biker is getting closer. Cole presses harder on the gas. He hits eighty MPH. The old van seems to cap at this speed.

Streetlights and storefronts rush by outside the windows. Ahead a Mazda turns onto Main. It coasts around the speed limit, thirty-five. Cole swerves over a yellow line around it, into the path of oncoming traffic. The heavy crates of drugs slam into the van's wall with a whump.

A GMC Yukon, its horn honking, drives toward the van. Cole rips his steering wheel to the right, zipping back over the yellow line, cutting off the Mazda.

Ahead he sees a stop sign. Nearby, a trio of teenage girls leaves the movie theater. They step into the street to cross.

Cole punches his horn. The girls snap their heads to him. One squeals. They backpedal onto the sidewalk as he blows through the stop sign.

He ticks the van back up to eighty MPH. He checks his mirror. The biker is still on his tail. His Harley is fast, gaining ground.

The biker's vest flaps as he goes about a hundred. He veers left and vanishes into Cole's blind spot.

The Harley rides up to the van's driver-side window. A tattoo of the Grim Reaper is on the biker's neck.

His eyes lock with Cole's. The guy reaches under his vest and points a revolver at Cole's face.

Cole throws his torso onto the van's passenger seat, losing all visibility of the road.

The driver-side window shatters, a bullet piercing it. A split second later the round fractures the passenger-side window, shards of glass spraying onto Cole's cheek.

Cole tries to keep the wheel steady with just his left hand. A bullet hits a tire. The van slants into the next lane, the drug crates banging around in the back.

A horn blares. Another vehicle must be coming at Cole head-on.

He spins the wheel right and rumbles back into his lane. The oncoming car whooshes by. But the van wobbles, about to tip.

Cole lifts his foot from the gas. The van rotates clockwise, slivers of broken glass pattering on the floor.

The spinning stops. The van idles on a diagonal across its lane.

The motorcycle engine revs.

Cole grasps the pistol in his jeans. He edges his head just above his steering wheel. The biker charges at him, aiming the revolver. He spiderwebs the van's windshield. The bullet misses Cole by inches and clangs a back door.

Cole tries aiming through the busted driver-side window, but the Harley blurs past, out of sight.

He straightens his wheel and presses the gas. He puts on his seatbelt.

In the mirror, the biker chases him. Cole only goes about fifty, letting the guy ride up to him. Cole watches him in the mirror, seeing him disappear into his blind spot like he did before.

Cole anticipates the biker will try the same move again, zoom up to his window on the left and try to shoot him.

Cole pounds the gas while angling the van left. Then he nails the brake.

The back of the van rattles. Cole's torso lurches against the belt across his chest.

He resettles in his seat and straightens the van. In the mirror, the Harley is toppled on the asphalt. The biker crawls to it with slow, pained movements. His gun lies a few feet away.

Cole turns the van around and runs over the motorcycle, pulverizing its front fork.

"You piece of shit," the biker yells.

Cole backs up, crushing the Harley's rear wheel, then speeds away.

19

One hand on the wheel of the van, Cole writes an email on his phone to his Army Ranger friend Owen, who now works at the DEA in Washington, DC. Attached to the message is the drug-evidence video Cole just took. In the body of the email, he includes a request to forward his message to the head of the Billings, Montana DEA office, plus the number of his burner phone. He hits send.

He thinks of Melanie and Powaw. Anticipating a potential backlash after the seizure of the drugs, he advised them to spend the night at the home of Melanie's college friend who lives a couple towns over. He admitted he was after justice for Jay, but to prevent panic, left out many details.

He searches for Melanie's contact on his burner and calls her. Ringing for a while. No answer. He calls Powaw.

"Hello?" the old man says.

Cole lowers the balaclava under his chin. "It's me. Those bikers responsible for Jay's coma, a few of them saw me take something of theirs. To get it back, they're almost certain to come after you guys, try to intimidate you so I hand it over."

A long silence on the other line. "Oh, Cole."

"It sounds bad, I know. But it'll all be over soon when the DEA cracks down on them. Stay where you are. Don't leave, not even for a minute, until I give you the green light. Mel's not picking up. Fill her in without freaking her out, then—"

"That won't be easy. I'll see what I can do. We'll check in soon."

"Thanks. Use this number, not my normal one. So long, Pop."

Cole ends the call. He travels a meandering mountain road back up to Banshee Point and parks in the clearing he did earlier. The light from his phone, tucked under his chin, provides some visibility.

He unloads the two narcotics crates and drags them into the forest by their handles. Pulling the one on his right irritates his fractured rib.

Unlike his last trip here, he does not descend to the water, but hikes to the high point, passing a cliff on his left.

He tips one crate, emptying the clear packages of pills, careful not to tear any on the terrain's sharp rocks, then dumps the second.

He grabs a flat rock about the size of a shoebox lid and, applying it like a shovel, scoops out a clump of earth.

The ground is stubborn. Digging makes his knuckles, wrists, and elbows sore. He needs almost an hour to deepen the hole enough. He buries the drugs and pats down the dirt, leveling it.

Despite the near-freezing temperature, he sweats from the brow. He dabs it with his forearm. With the Google Maps app on his burner phone, he looks up the latitude/longitude of the buried drugs and takes a screenshot.

He stows the empty crates in the van and gets in the driver's seat. The street value of the narcotics must be over two million dollars. Every Freedom Rider must be looking for him.

If Cole left the woods, they could spot him in the noticeable Harris Meats van. He shouldn't even turn on the heat. Running the engine could attract attention. He'll endure the cold all night, without sleep.

If they find him, he'll be ready. He reaches to the back of his jeans and grips the .45.

20

Cole slides Earl's phone from his pocket. He scrolls through its text message history with contact *Russell Garnold*.

Earlier today Russell sent Earl Cole's address, plus the message: *Make sure the prick doesn't stop by the vine ever again. He seems to have some kind of training. Ambush his ass.*

Cole scrolls deeper back into their text history, spotting various orders about picking up and dropping off what must be drugs, referenced in ambiguous code terms, *birthday gifts*, *Christmas gifts*, *anniversary gifts*.

Three times within the last six months, Russell mentions someone he calls *Gator*. Cole eyes the most recent instance: *If we don't get these Xmas presents moving by Thursday, Gator is gonna be pissed.* In all three cases, Russell speaks with deference as if underneath this person in a chain of command.

Based on the value of the drugs, the Freedom Riders aren't running some small-time dope ring. They could be distributors for a bigger operation this Gator controls.

Cole's opposition may be larger than the ten bikers.

His regular phone vibrates, *Sgt. Sandra Evans* calling. He lowers the facial covering and answers.

"What's up, Sergeant?" he asks.

"Motorcycles are flying around downtown with men in Freedom Riders vests on them. They're checking out all the alleys like they're searching for someone. You happen to know anything about this, Mister Maddox?"

"You think they're looking for me?"

"Well, your Jeep is on fire. The fire department is on Main hosing it down as we speak. I thought you were heading right to your cabin after I saw you?"

He taps the van's steering wheel with the barrel of the gun. He can't keep evading her by playing dumb. He should give her a partial truth.

"Look, I have a confession to make," he says.

"That so?"

"I did some investigating of my own. And heard the Freedom Riders were behind Jay's attack. I said something to them at The Knotted Vine. They didn't like it. The attempted robbery at my place must've been some sort of retaliation."

"I figured the story went something like that."

"Sorry I kept it from you. I didn't want you to think I was stepping on your case."

"Where are you?"

"A safe spot."

She is quiet for a bit. "It may not be safe for long with an entire gang searching for you. Come to the police station. It's the securest spot in Timber Ridge. Spend the night there while my team tries to talk some sense into the bikers, calm things down. I have a couch in my office."

A pleasant surprise. He assumed she was going to grill him about his lies. But his safety seems to be of more concern.

"Thanks for the offer," he says, "but I'd have to pass through downtown to get to the station. They could notice."

"I'll send an officer to pick you up."

He considers the possibility of a biker anticipating this move, following the police cruiser to Banshee Point, and finding the drugs. He should head somewhere else to meet the cop. Someplace quiet, accessible from back roads.

In the distance, he sees the old Hadaway factory.

21

Its lights off, Cole's commandeered van coasts along a dark dirt road. A lone headlight beam emerges on the horizon, approaching via a paved street on the other side of the woods. The sound of a Harley engine accompanies it.

The biker passes without noticing the van opposite the trees. But maybe he'll check the dirt road next.

Cole, not far from the Hadaway building, opts to complete the trip on foot. He pulls over into the brush, leaves covering the van. He destroys Earl's phone with a rock and pockets his own, the regular and burner.

The wind rams into him as he moves toward the factory's rear through dense forest. After hiking about half a mile, he reaches a fence and climbs it. The movement exacerbates the pain from his broken rib. He lands on the other side of the chain links and ascends a hill, the only heat in his body the burning in his thighs.

The incline sharpens toward the peak. Gripping tree barks for support, he negotiates the slope onto flat ground.

For a couple seconds, he catches his breath, wisping in front of him in the cold with the balaclava under his chin.

Now that he's here, about to unite with the cops, he must get rid of the biker's pistol. Its serial number is scratched off. For all he knows, it's been used in multiple murders. Not the type of belonging to tote inside a police station. He wipes the gun clean of prints with his tee shirt, then drops it and kicks it into the woods.

Kneeling behind a bush, he peers at an asphalt expanse behind the building. A large, faded sign says, *Parking for the Hadaway Family of Employees.* No bikers lurk in the lot, but they could show up. Just in case, he packed an alternative weapon in his jeans, a tire iron from the van's spare-tire kit.

The cop, traveling via automobile versus foot, should already be out front. Cole heads there. The big juniper trees around the property sway in the wind.

He glimpses the spray-painted words on the building's rear, which he assumes are from disgruntled ex-employees. *Blow Me, Greedy Scum, Traitors.*

His burner vibrates. Melanie.

He answers. "You and Quinn good?"

"We're fine."

"I'm sorry for getting us into this. But it was the only way to keep the guys who hurt Jay away from us for good. I'll explain everything at a better time."

"I believe you. Speaking of the men who hurt Jay, wait till you hear this. When you called me before, I didn't pick up because I was in the middle of a pretty weird chat on the internet."

"With who?"

"I wound up making that GoFundMe page for Jay's medical bills, like you told me to. I posted the link on Facebook to get the word out. And one of my friends must be friends with one of her friends or...however Facebook does it...and Diane Nolan winds up seeing my post."

"Who?"

"The wife of Lawrence Nolan, the guy who runs the antique store across from the alley where Jay was chased. So she comments on my post, says something like, did the cops arrest anyone yet? And I write her back, still working on it, too bad we didn't see anything on your video. Then she goes, what about the man on the motorcycle?"

"What man?"

"Apparently his back is to the camera. You can't make out his face. But Diane said you can clearly see Jay on the sidewalk. And this guy pulls up to him on a bike. Jay keeps walking, out of the frame. And this guy follows him. You can't see the alley, no footage of anything violent. But still, this seems like quality evidence."

"Certainly does."

"That sergeant who saw the surveillance tape, Evans, didn't mention anything to you about a man on a bike?"

"No."

"Is this cop leading Jay's case even competent?"

"Cole," Sandra Evans calls out. Waving, she approaches him from the front of the building.

"Let me call you back," he says to Melanie. He hangs up. And walks to Sandra. His hand inches toward the tire iron in case she makes a move on him. "What happened with the antique store's security—"

A rifle roars off to his side. A bullet rips through him.

22

Cole falls to his back, a bullet sizzling in his chest. A crimson oval balloons on his white tee shirt. Sandra does not seem surprised.

A male silhouette emerges from behind a tree with a rifle in its arms. Pointing the weapon at Cole, the man yells, "Hands in the air."

Catching his breath, Cole rises to his knees. Blood flows from his left pectoral muscle onto the pavement. He was shot in the upper chest, just in from his shoulder. Despite the pain, no vital organ was hit.

If they wanted him dead, they would've fired again. Or aimed for the head on the first blast. If they need him alive, their next move will be restraining him.

Cole lifts his hands in the air. The male approaches, late thirties, black goatee. He wears a Timber Ridge Police Department uniform.

"On your feet, asshole," he says.

Cole stands. Sandra, shining a flashlight on him, pulls the phones from his pockets and pats him down. Before she reaches the tire iron, Cole does.

He launches it over Sandra's shoulder at the other cop. The guy blocks his face with the rifle. The tool clanks against the gun. The cop backpedals.

Cole darts around Sandra at the guy. Cole goes for the rifle, but the cop slams the butt into Cole's elbow. The men collide. And fall to the pavement.

The policeman sits up and aims the gun at Cole's shoulder. But Cole grasps the barrel, angles it away. Cole stands. The cop's front hand is wrapped around the rifle's wooden fore-end. Cole kicks it, crunching the cop's fingers. His proximal phalanx bones snap.

The moaning policeman's grip loosens. Cole yanks the weapon from him. The officer's eyes panicky, he reaches for the pistol at his waist while Cole points the rifle down at him.

The cop unholsters his sidearm, but Cole gets a shot off first. At such close range, chunks of skull and brain spurt onto Cole's boots.

He whips the gun around at Sandra, who points her pistol at him with shaky hands.

"You can't kill me," Cole says. "You need me to tell you where the drugs are, right?"

She says nothing.

"I can kill you though," he says.

"Please. Please, Cole. I had no choice."

He laughs.

"It wasn't supposed to be like this," she says. "I had a peaceful business arrangement going on with the bikers. Until you had to show up in town and get involved. If I didn't lure you into this trap for them, they threatened to slit my throat."

"What about the Timber Ridge parents at teenage funerals because of ODs? You call that a peaceful arrangement?"

"What about Earl Laughlin? He still hasn't turned up. Will he be needing a funeral because of you? Then the two others at the butcher shop. Beaten almost to death. Another left on Main with a concussion, broken leg and arm. Is that your idea of peace?"

He steps to her, snatches the pistol out of her hand, and slips it in his pocket.

"Seems you're okay with lawlessness if it's for revenge," she says. "You break the law for your brother. I break it for myself. Is there a difference?"

Killing her would be advantageous. But since she's not trying to hurt him, the act would not be self-defense.

He handcuffs her to a handicap sign on a parking space, then collects her flashlight, radio, cuff and car keys, and phone. He strips off the male cop's jacket and puts it on for warmth, covering his white tee shirt, the entire left half soaked in blood.

"Thank you for letting me live," she says. "Now let me return the favor. You have no idea what you're up against. The bikers are the least of the problems coming for you. Don't go any farther down this path. Give back the drugs and save yourself."

He slings the rifle over his shoulder and removes both his phones from Sandra's coat. His regular one, registered with a national telecom company, can be traced by authorities. He hurls it into the woods, pockets his burner, and trots toward the front of the building.

If he doesn't control his bleeding soon, he'll pass out, becoming an easy target for a biker, crooked cop, or whatever else may be looming.

23

Cole rides the county highway in the Timber Ridge cop car Sandra took to the factory. Before getting in, he grabbed a compression trauma bandage from the first-aid kit in the trunk. It's limited his blood loss, but he's spilled enough to become dizzy. He should go to a hospital, but they could be waiting for him there.

He heads toward Ripsaw Mountain, a small ski destination in Danesville, about forty-five minutes outside Timber Ridge. He and Jay have been going to the mountain since elementary school, when their biological parents taught them to ski.

Soon a tall peak emerges on the horizon. Cole cruises into an area where he's stayed before, rental properties and second homes scattered by the base of the mountain. Mid-October, ski season still about a month away, he figures a good number of the houses will be unoccupied.

He coasts past a home, a car in the driveway. Past another, the glow of a TV through a sheer curtain.

At the third house, no cars, windows dark. He pulls over and peeks through a side window with a view into the foyer, a buildup of mail under the door slot. A framed photograph hangs on the wall of a couple in their seventies surrounded by six grandchildren. Nobody seems home. A vacation house not in use tonight.

It has a garage, but Cole doesn't have another hanger, so he breaks a rear window with his elbow, out of sight from the neighbors. He unlocks it and enters the shadowy residence.

He pulls the police cruiser into the garage. In the flame of the stove, he disinfects a set of tweezers from the first-aid kit, then brings them upstairs with tubes of antibiotic and medical glue, plus the rifle.

He strips off his clothing and bandage in the master bathroom. In the mirror, he gazes at the red wound on his upper chest. Wincing, he plunges the tweezers into it and feels around for the bullet. Jolts of pain cut through his left arm to the wrist. He plucks out the projectile.

It chimes against the sink. He tosses it out the window and runs water to wash away the streaks of blood on the porcelain.

A hot shower provides a bit of relief to his aching body. He cleans his wound and the rest of himself and dries off. After dabbing antibiotic in his torn skin and sealing it with the glue the best he can, he re-bandages, re-dresses, and sits on the edge of the master bedroom's mattress with the rifle.

The window offers an elevated angle to blast down on his enemies if they have the luck to find this house, and the brashness to approach.

He may not yet know whom he is up against.

But neither do they.

24

Real estate developer Wayne Shaw sits beside his wife at an oak dining table at the home of their friends, the Dodsworths, a couple who lives near them on Mohawk Trail, Timber Ridge's priciest street. Among the four fiftysomethings are three empty bottles of Opus One Cabernet and a fourth about halfway done. A large oil painting of a bison herd hangs on the wall.

Like Wayne, Ken Dodsworth inherited his money. Unlike Wayne, his wealth isn't affected by Timber Ridge's current economic hardships. Ken's father was a logistics executive at the Hadaway factory. When the company went public in 1991, his stock options turned into a couple million bucks, which he pumped into a thriving mutual fund. Upon his father's death, Ken inherited a ten-figure sum that's grown since.

In his big seat at the head of the table, Ken leans toward Wayne's wife, Adeline. She has short brown hair, crow's feet, and a slight sag to the skin under her chin. With a carefree smile, Ken tells a story about an outing on the golf course. "So I hit a good one, the kind of swing where you can just hear it. You know…ping."

"I don't really golf," Adeline says. "But yeah, ping, I get it."

"So I'm watching the fairway. Waiting to see the ball sail, bounce in place for a birdie. But no. Never happened."

"Uh-oh."

He swirls his wine. "The ball exploded. Right there on my tee."

Adeline laughs while glancing at Ken's laughing wife, then asks, "Like literally, or is that some sports term?"

"Literally," Ken says. "Turns out it was a prank. Roger, my financial adviser, slipped some gag ball in my bag, designed to burst on impact. That son of a bitch got me good. I can imagine my face." He puts on an exaggerated expression of confusion.

Laughing harder than before, Adeline turns to Wayne for a reaction. He offers a small grin.

He isn't in the mood for jokes. Not since receiving a series of daunting messages on his phone during this dinner party, which he cannot share with the group, not even his wife.

Intensifying his stress is that Goddamn Dodsworth daughter, a twenty-year-old visiting home from college for a few days. Wearing yoga pants and a Montana State tee shirt, the pretty blonde bends over in the adjoining kitchen for a bottle of water. Wayne sneaks a glimpse of her heart-shaped ass.

He chugs the rest of his wine. Though he's happy to be married to Adeline, he's struggled with temptation in the presence of younger, better-looking women. He made a couple mistakes in the past she doesn't know about. But those days are over. Keeping his family intact is more important than satisfying these desires.

His phone vibrates. He checks the screen. A new message sent to him on an encrypted app: *Call me ASAP.*

Son of a bitch.

"Excuse me," he announces to the table. "I need to make a quick call for work. Something came up at Valley Gate." He stands.

Ken says, "For a problem to come up, doesn't the development need at least one tenant?"

Ken's wife rolls her eyes. "Honey."

"Wayne, buddy, I'm just joking," Ken says. "He knows that. He knows it."

Wayne smiles. "I do. It was…funny." He exits the dining room and passes through the kitchen and den, a deer-antler chandelier suspended from the twenty-foot ceiling. Through double doors, he walks onto a large back deck with a sprawling view of Timber Ridge.

He makes a voice-over-IP call with his encrypted app. Waiting for an answer, he paces in his gator-skin cowboy boots.

Russell, leader of the Freedom Riders, says over the phone, "We, eh, we still haven't located the missing stuff."

"Christ," Wayne says, keeping his voice down. He only paid up front for half the drugs, the other given to him on credit by his supplier, a debt to be paid back after the bikers sold the stash. If they don't find it, Wayne still owes the money. "I thought you said our friends in the police department were supposed—"

"They shot him. But he—"

"Shot him? I thought they were going to just…threaten him."

"After what he did to our three boys downtown, they wanted him incapacitated before they approached. It didn't work. One of my men just checked out the factory. This Maddox guy killed Yarvey, cuffed Sandra, and got away."

Wayne feels light-headed. He had moral qualms about getting into the opioid business, aware of the product's high overdose risk. However, he reasoned that the users were aware of the risk too. Wayne isn't forcing anyone to consume the product. If a user took a bad dose, the death would be his own fault, not Wayne's.

The justification may not make perfect sense, but Wayne swallowed it. He needed the damn money. Valley Gate, his large, upscale community of townhouses, his big bet, was finished just as Hadaway announced the shutdown of its factory. Amid the financial turmoil, Timber Ridge citizens shied away from upgrading to the expensive homes. Wayne is still bleeding cash to the bank every month.

Now that this business turned bloody, his feelings of guilt grow heavier. Cole Maddox shot. Officer Rick Yarvey dead. With his debt, Wayne can't just walk away from this. He needs to resolve it before more people are hurt.

"There's one of him and eleven of you guys," Wayne says. "I heard Cole's just some paper-pusher inspector. I'm sure you can figure out where he went and get everything back."

"He's more than that. I've squared up against plenty of dudes in my time, but this guy, he's…this is something different. And I'm pretty sure there's only ten of us now. His doing."

Wayne steps to the railing and stares down at the town his family began. Most of his wealth is tied up in land, which isn't liquid. He doesn't have a million dollars in cash lying around to cover his debt to his supplier, a Mexican cartel.

The cartel must've faced dilemmas like this before. They have a significant financial reason to resolve this one.

"I'll call Ernesto," Wayne says. "See if he can lend us a hand."

25

The dull light of a dreary morning hangs over Danesville, the small town where Cole's been hiding. A soft rain mists the bedroom window. Though his enemies haven't found him, he remains vigilant with his rifle in hand, watching for cops, bikers, or something worse.

A bit after seven AM, his burner phone vibrates. A call from a 406 area code, Billings, Montana.

He answers. "This is Cole."

"Hey Cole. Agent Ramirez with the DEA."

Cole stands. "Thanks for getting back to me."

"No, thank you. My boss just forwarded me that video you took. If what was in those crates is what you say it is, the street value is more than anything we've come across in a good minute. I want it ASAP."

"Bear with me if I'm a bit distrustful. I can't be sure you're a fed just because you dropped Owen's name. Do me a favor, reply to my email you were forwarded with the word 'okay.' I just want to see if you have a DEA dot gov email address so I know you're legit."

"Hang on."

Cole sees an email come in from Steven Ramirez, *okay* from a DEA.gov email address. Cole responds with the screenshot of the drugs' latitude/longitude.

"Just sent you the location of the buried drugs," Cole says. "I've got a bit of heat on me that'll only go away when you guys snag everything and I'm no longer a human treasure map."

"Your pal Owen said you were tough." He whistles. "But damn. Taking down those bikers, taking that much product off them. Yeah, I'm sure they're still a tad miffed. We've got your back though."

"Appreciate it. If you leave Billings now, you can get to the spot a little after ten AM."

"Well, here's the thing. When I say I want the stuff ASAP, I mean today, but not this morning. Our office has been working two big undercover cases near Helena. I've got surveillance obligations up here all morning and afternoon. My partner and I will make the trek down to you as soon as we break for the day. You'll see us tonight."

"Hmm."

"That an issue?"

"Last night these people shot me. I already lost a good amount of blood and can't go to a hospital until you guys cool things down for me."

"Man. Wish I could send someone sooner. But we operate out of Billings. Not Miami, New York, or LA. No agents on standby for anything that short notice."

Cole paces. "All right. Tonight, then."

"Look, if you need medical help, call the cops in Timber Ridge. They can escort you to a hospital, stand guard while the doc treats the blood loss."

"A good idea in theory. But the cops in Timber Ridge were the ones who shot me."

"God."

"A sergeant, Sandra Evans, is on the payroll of the drug dealers, maybe more."

"Wow. Okay."

"Once you get it all in an evidence locker in Billings, it would help if you did a press release. Make sure these people know the DEA has their stuff, not me."

"Happy to smile on camera in front of a couple mill of confiscated opioids."

Cole would think Sandra concocted some lie about him killing her colleague and stealing her car. If so, he's facing a police-officer murder charge. Every cop in the state should have his photo and be after him. The only way for the problem to disappear is exposing Sandra and any cronies as crooked.

"It would be great if you guys could look into this Sergeant Evans this morning," Cole says. "Even if you're in Helena, you can put in a request for her phone records. Possibly—"

"You were distrustful of me. And it's my job to be distrustful of you. Until I get my hands on what you buried, test it, and verify it's what you say it is, I don't have the authority to start investigating anyone."

Cole sits back on the bed. "I understand."

"See you tonight."

"Sounds good."

Cole hangs up. And takes a deep breath. He's optimistic about his new ally Agent Ramirez, but not the blood-loss-induced dizziness in his head. Twelve hours, maybe more, could pass before the DEA arrives. If Cole can't go to a hospital during that stretch, he'll at least need to replenish himself with food.

Last night he drank a few cups of sink water from a kitchen glass, but ate nothing, the refrigerator and pantry empty. If he hunkered down all day without eating, he could faint. If his enemies happened to track him here in that state, he'd be done for.

He searches on his phone for "delivery food near me." Nothing is available in this little ski village off-season at this early hour. He remembers once eating breakfast at a bagel shop not far from here. He can't risk going inside, exposing his face to the public. But maybe he can find some scraps in the garbage out back.

He opens the bedroom closet. A few women's sweaters on hangers. A couple men's flannel shirts beside them. He removes his bloodstained tee shirt and puts one on.

Downstairs, he finds an umbrella in a closet. Keeping it low to mask his face, he sets off on foot with Sandra's pistol concealed in his jeans.

Each step twinges his cracked rib. The rain patters on his umbrella over the three-mile journey on hilly dirt roads, woods all around.

He spots the bagel shop. No other businesses are on this street leading to Ripsaw Mountain except a ski-rental place, a gas station, and a closed bar.

He turns behind the bagel shop, yanks a bag out of a trash can, and rips it open. Chunks of gnawed food and dirty napkins fall onto the pavement. He looks for bagel morsels with egg, which is known to revitalize red blood cells. He devours a piece. Then another. And another. Energy courses through his depleted body.

Behind him, he hears a rustling noise. A black bear walks out of the woods.

It could've smelled the food.

Sudden movements could provoke it, so Cole stands still. "Hi big fella," he says in a calm voice. "Eat all you want." He takes slow steps away from the food.

The bear's eyes follow him. The animal seems more interested in Cole than the bagel scraps. Cole glances at his chest. A couple red dots seep through his shirt. The walk here must've reopened his wound a bit. The bear smells blood.

Cole takes another slow step toward the dirt road. The bear steps in the same direction. Then walks toward Cole. Its legs move faster. Even faster.

No way Cole can outrun it. He grabs Sandra's pistol and shoots it in the leg. The gunshot booms through the quiet neighborhood. The bear staggers back toward the woods.

But the rear door of the bagel shop flies open. A man in an apron peers outside. He notices Cole with a pistol. The door slams, the man vanishing.

Cole throws aside the umbrella and sprints back toward the house.

26

Adeline Shaw pours herself fresh orange juice at her breakfast table, in a sunroom off her and Wayne's kitchen. Though the sun isn't out, the daylight still brings out all the age lines on her makeup-less face. Across from her, Wayne sips coffee, already on his third cup. He didn't sleep much last night, awoken by a nightmare of a faceless figure chasing him through the Valley Gate townhouse development.

"I really hope Jackson does all right on that pre-calc test today," Adeline says.

She spoons berries from an artisanal bowl they bought while vacationing in Switzerland, then glimpses her husband as if for a reaction to her comment about their son. He says nothing, his eyes out the window at the rainy view of downtown from Mohawk Trail. The storefronts and cars appear small and fake from this height.

"Honey?" Adeline says.

"Jackson. Yes."

"He said he was studying all night."

"Right."

"He's starting to stress about college." She sighs. "I don't blame him. Junior year was the toughest for me too."

"It'll, you know, it'll work out."

She sips her juice. "I was talking to him a couple nights ago about college and his future. Know what he told me? That he wants to be just like you. Work under you at the family company when he graduates. Learn. Turn into a big businessman someday like his dad."

Wayne coughs. Again. He doesn't stop.

"Here," Adeline says, rushing to fill a glass with water. He gulps it. "You okay?"

He forces a smile.

After breakfast, Adeline stands and kisses his cheek. "I'm going to change for tennis."

He squeezes her arm. She wanders up to the second level. He descends to the basement.

The sunlight from the first floor dissolves into the heavy shadows down here. He paces to the back of the room and turns on an overhead lamp, illuminating a game area. His son Jackson's air hockey and ping-pong tables sit near a circus-themed pinball machine Wayne's parents bought him for Christmas when he was nine.

The machine has comforted Wayne since childhood. For the last year or so, he's played it to ease himself before heading into the office, where he spends most of the day peering at Excel spreadsheets outlining how deep his financial hole is.

Pudoot, he ejects the silver ball with the plunger. *Blahding.* He whacks it with a flipper. *Voink, voink.*

His phone vibrates in his sweatpants. He checks the screen. Ernesto, his contact from the cartel, is calling through the encrypted app. Wayne left him a voicemail last night about the Cole Maddox predicament.

Wayne answers. "Hey."

"I am glad you contacted me about this issue instead of trying to resolve it yourself," Ernesto says in his Mexican accent. "These men on the motorbikes, they may be good at giving a product to a customer and collecting money. And these police may be good at collecting money from you and not arresting the men on the motorbikes. But those are quite different tasks than the one at hand."

Wayne twirls the drawstring of his sweats around his finger. "So you have an idea for tracking down this Maddox guy?"

"Help is already on the way via airplane from Texas."

"Oh. Okay then."

"My colleague has been placed in similar circumstances. With a positive result. It goes without saying, but I will say it anyway, his compensation will come from your end, not mine."

"I…uh…yeah, of course."

"But, rest assured, he is only compensated if he uncovers what he is looking for. His fee is a cut of the profits once sold."

"He's confident in his abilities. I like that."

"He has reason to be confident. He is the best I've ever seen at the task at hand. When he arrives in Montana, connect him with the people who've failed so far. Have them brief him on whatever they know, and be ready to assist if he calls on them for anything."

"So what makes him so good at this type of thing?"

"His father comes from my country. But his mother is an American woman, just as White as you. He grew up in the US, fought for the American army. A Navy SEAL. Did work like this in Afghanistan. Were you aware the country is the world's top cultivator of opium? The poppy plant substance used to make what we sell."

"I…no, I was not aware."

"During the war, the Americans' official position was that

they would devastate Afghanistan's opium production. But despite its ability to do so, the army never did."

"Why not?"

"Nobody ever destroys something of value. They may slice it up. But only to divvy it out. A poppy field is no exception. Some in the US Army made quite a deal of money during that war. For themselves and their friends. My associate thrived at locating high-value goods local farmers would move into hiding. He was paid off Uncle Sam's books of course."

"Huh."

"He lands in two hours. Do not miss his call."

"What is this man's name?"

"A man, he is, yes." Ernesto is silent for a moment. "But I consider him something more than that. A leveling force. Like a great flood or great fire. He may cause harm. But in the aftermath will be a new beginning. A new peace. He is called Angel."

Wayne twirls his drawstring even tighter around his finger. "Thank…thank you for arranging this."

"Some of his methods may make a man like you somewhat uncomfortable. But do not question him. Is that understood?"

Wayne is already uncomfortable. "Yeah, understood."

27

A Danesville police cruiser drives over a hill. Cole stops running, his feet slipping on the muddy dirt road. The car's lights and siren come on. Cole turns around and runs through the rain the way he came.

If he is arrested, and the drug dealers happened to kidnap Melanie, Quinn, or Powaw, jailed Cole couldn't rescue them. A dirty cop may even torture him in a private cell for the pills' location.

He cuts into the brush. The police car skids to a halt. An officer jumps out and chases him while the driver continues down the road.

The woods in this residential area are somewhat thin. If Cole is going to lose these cops, he'll have to reach the vast wilderness behind Ripsaw Mountain.

"Stop," the policeman shouts.

Cole doesn't. He runs full speed for about a quarter mile. Over his shoulder, he sees the pursuing cop has fallen behind.

When the trees end, Cole finds himself in a backyard. He climbs the fence onto the neighbor's property. A woman working out inside eyes him through the sliding-glass door.

He climbs another fence and lands on a tricycle. He slips, twisting his ankle, but gets back up and keeps running, though not as fast. Down the hill, the block intersects with the street leading to the ski mountain.

Cole turns onto it. A few seconds later, so does the cop car.

Cole darts into the alley behind the closed bar. The car stops. The driver chases him. He's quicker than his partner. Cole approaches a fence topped with a coil of barbed wire. He tucks his hands into the sleeves of his flannel and climbs.

Razors rip through his shirt, stabbing his palms, stomach, thighs. He hops down to the other side, blood sprinkling off him, and races out of the alley onto the street.

Another siren. A second cop car zooms toward him.

Cole notices a man filling up a Cadillac at the gas station across the street and runs to him. The guy steps backward with a scared expression. Cole yanks open the Cadillac's passenger door and jumps inside.

He sits behind the steering wheel and keeps the door open until the officer catches up and sees him.

Cole slams the passenger door, opens the driver's, and crawls out of the car. He peeks beneath it. The cop reverses his cruiser, trying to block the gas station's pathway onto the road. As Cole intended, the officer thinks he's about to drive off in the Cadillac.

Instead, crouching Cole scurries around the gas pumps and disappears from the cop's view on the back side of the ski-rental shop.

He dashes through the woods bordering the road. He soon sees the sign for *Ripsaw Mountain* and enters its parking lot.

Though the mountain isn't open in October for skiing, it is for hiking. Patrol staff should be present, along with their requisite vehicles.

Cole runs to a hut, on it *Ski Patrol* and a red cross. A few all-terrain vehicles are lined up outside. Their keys are already in their ignitions for quick access in case of an emergency.

He jumps on one and turns it on. The engine purrs.

A guy about nineteen scampers out from the hut, the mountain logo on his windbreaker. "Yo homie, those aren't for the public."

"I know. Sorry." Cole squeezes the throttle and blazes past him up the mountain.

28

A shuttle from Bozeman Yellowstone Airport pulls up to a rental-car lot. Passengers exit. Among them is thirty-six-year-old Angel, the only one without luggage. His six-foot-four frame is cloaked in black. Boots, jeans, shirt, and a duster cover his muscular two hundred twenty-five pounds. His green eyes, inherited from his White mother, are set against a light-brown complexion passed down from his Hispanic father.

He chooses a rental car that won't stand out on the road, a silver Toyota Corolla, and pays with an alias credit card, its name also on the phony driver's license he presents. He embarks on the trip south humming a tune, admiring the mountainous Montana scenery.

In about an hour, a *Welcome to Timber Ridge* sign materializes on the horizon. He drives a quiet street toward a public park where he's scheduled to meet Wayne. But coasts to a stop when a brawny, middle-aged man wanders into the road after a dog. He has greasy blond hair and a coat with holes. The tent nearby could be his home.

Angel gives his horn a polite tap.

The vagrant spins his head to him. "Gimme a second, asshole."

Angel does not reply. The man struggles to gather the quick terrier shuffling back and forth across both the road's lanes. Angel gives him half a minute, then taps his horn again.

The vagrant turns to him, grabs his groin, and shakes it.

Angel shifts the car into park and exits into the drizzle. "Could you kindly move out of the road, sir?"

The vagrant's eyes narrow as they take in Angel's imposing stature. The vagrant tucks his hand under his tattered coat, suggesting he's armed, and says, "I don't know what country you're from, Pedro. But here in America, here in Montana, if a man confronts you, you've got all sorts of rights to stand your ground. I'd get back in that car if I were you and drive the way you came."

Angel peers into his eyes without blinking.

A click, the cocking of a pistol hammer. Angel's hand flies under the vagrant's coat and pries the weapon from him. He points it at the man's forehead.

The vagrant cowers, his hands up in surrender. "Don't. I'm sorry." He scurries off the pavement onto the grass. "Drive wherever you want, please."

Angel enjoys watching this. Human beings on the cusp of death intrigue him. He studies the details of the vagrant's face, the twitching of his cheek muscles, the dryness of his lips, the sweat accumulating on his hairline. Angel wonders what he's thinking in this moment. Maybe of all his dreams. Maybe of all his regrets.

Angel holds the gun on him until hearing an engine around the bend. He lowers the pistol.

Though Angel would relish killing him, another passing motorist could witness. Angel will let him keep his life, but would not feel right if he didn't rob him of something.

Angel bends down and whistles with a melodic rhythm. The

small dog runs to him. He picks it up and says, "If the police happen to question me about this incident, I will know you sent them. And I will find you." He sets the dog on the passenger seat of the Toyota.

"What're you doing with her?" the vagrant asks.

"Don't worry. I'll give her a good home." Angel sits behind his wheel and closes the door.

The vagrant drops to his knees crying.

Angel drives for a couple miles. He snaps the animal's neck. Then lowers a window and tosses the carcass onto the roadside dirt.

29

Cole mounts the stolen all-terrain vehicle, or ATV, in the wilderness behind Ripsaw Mountain.

He's been on the run for over two hours. A couple ski-patrol employees spotted him in the brush, but Cole got away. Then a pair of cops tracked him down. Cole ditched them, but lost the pistol in his waist during the turbulent ATV ride. He also burned a lot of gas, his tank now almost on *E*.

His eyes scan the vicinity for movement. Nothing but birds and squirrels.

Then a dog barks.

A couple hundred feet down the hill, a German shepherd watches Cole through the foliage. Cole worked with the breed on army missions. The dog can pick up a scent from over a mile away. This one must've just sniffed him out.

The man holding its leash, in the brown-and-tan uniform of the County Sheriff's Office, gazes in the same direction as it.

Cole turns the ATV's key, its motor coming back to life. He descends the hill opposite the cop and canine. His wheels rumble over the rocky terrain for about a mile.

He hears a second engine. Beyond the trees, another ATV is

on the county road. It swings toward him, atop it a thirtyish redheaded policeman with mean eyes.

Cole skids to a stop, rocks kicking up from his tires as they quake across the uneven ground. He zooms away from his pursuer into a shallow stream.

Water splashes up at his ankles. The density of trees increases on the other side. He pivots his handlebars left, veering around one, then jerks them right, avoiding a bigger one. Spruce needles graze his forehead.

Over his shoulder, he sees the cop a couple dozen feet behind. Cole rotates his head forward. A flash in his periphery. Antlers. A deer dashes through the forest, about to collide with him.

Cole slams his brake, the rear of his ATV whipping counter-clockwise. The big deer sidesteps him, hurtling past. At a stop, Cole glances at the policeman barreling to him. Steering with one hand, he aims a gun at Cole with the other.

Fuchoot. An object sticks in a tree a few feet from Cole, a small metal shaft with a feathery red butt. A tranquilizer dart.

Cole punches his gas, banking left, zipping into an even tighter thicket of trees.

While he laces through the spruces, he scopes his fuel indicator, the red pin now touching the black line at *E.*

He decides to ride to the county road. Maybe the cop won't chase him with motorists around.

Cole charges through the stream, then over boulders. His elbow joints are tugged on as he tries to keep hold of the handlebars. He bolts between two pines onto asphalt and cruises the road's shoulder.

A sedan drives past him, wind gusting against Cole. Looking back, he sees the policeman continuing the chase, unfazed by the surrounding cars.

The cop, his ATV newer and faster, gains on Cole on the open road. The cop aims his tranq gun. Cole zigzags, making himself a difficult target. He cuts across the two-lane street into incoming traffic. A dump truck closes in on him, its horn bellowing.

Cole drives off the blacktop onto unkempt grass. The truck howls past. Cole yanks his handlebars around and rides alongside it.

His engine sputters. He glimpses the gas needle, now beneath the *E*.

He takes a deep breath and drives up to the truck's lift cylinder, the long hydraulic rod that causes the back to go up and down. His left hand clutches the rod, his right keeping the ATV steady. A raspy cough from his engine, nothing left in the tank.

He leaps off the ATV. He grabs the rod with his other hand. His abdomen bangs into the truck, deepening the split in his rib, abrading his rifle wound.

To keep his legs off the asphalt ripping by beneath him, he bends at the knees. His vacated ATV careens into a divot and flips.

With a grunt, he climbs upward, struggling to hang on at forty MPH, his shirt flapping. He hooks an arm around the dump box, stabilizing himself. The driver, who does not seem to recognize an addition to the back, keeps moving.

Soon the cop's ATV emerges behind the truck. Cole could heave rocks from the truck's load near him, shake him up, back him off the chase.

Just before he grips a rock, the officer shoots out a truck tire with his pistol. The driver hits the brake. The truck angles to the shoulder and stops.

Cole hops off, runs around the truck's nose, then across the blacktop into the other lane. A honking SUV swerves around him.

He re-enters the woods. Seconds later, so does the cop on the ATV. Cole's only hope is to somehow lose him in the woods on foot.

Fuchoot. A projectile impales a tree inches from Cole.

Offense may be his best defense. He tears the feathered object out of the bark.

The cop re-aims. Before he can shoot, Cole jumps at him and stabs the dart in his thigh.

"Son of a bitch," the officer yells.

He'll soon go woozy and pass out. He tries to grab his radio, but Cole does first and sprints away into the forest.

30

Angel pushes a shopping cart through an aisle of the Timber Ridge Home Depot, a black umbrella inside. He tosses in three wrenches, then moves to another aisle and drops in a roll of duct tape, next a bundle of rope and pack of zip ties, then shears, a wide-brim black booney hat, and a pair of work gloves.

He strolls to a register line. A little boy about six, in front of him with his dad, glimpses Angel. The child covers his face with a hand as if playing peek-a-boo. In a moment, he lowers it. Angel hides his own face with his hands, then opens his fingers, revealing an eye. The boy smiles.

Angel pays in cash and pockets the eighty-five cents change versus placing it in a donation tin near the register labeled *Wounded Veterans*.

He carries the bagged items into his rented Toyota, then undoes the umbrella's Velcro strap, its top billowing out. He secures the three wrenches to the umbrella shaft with zip ties and fastens the Velcro over them, yielding one of his favorite weapons.

Another deadly tool waits in the glovebox, a 9mm pistol with a silencer. Though he acquired a gun from that vagrant, he did not know its history, so wiped his prints off and disposed of it. He requested Wayne bring a sidearm with a clean serial number to their meeting in the park.

Angel drives to the home of Cole Maddox's brother, Jay, and his wife, Melanie. Wayne seemed squeamish giving the address, but did.

Angel streams a song from his phone through the stereo, "Magic Marker Tattoos," a pop hit about first love by eighteen-year-old sensation Crissy Rogue.

Soon he parks in the street in front of the house. Cole's brother is still comatose at the Gallatin Health Center in Bozeman, but Angel hopes the wife is home. In his experience, parents with young children are easy targets for information.

Angel rings the bell, the umbrella dangling at his side. No answer. He peeks through a window. Shadows. Nobody home.

He gets back in his car and goes to the next address Wayne provided, the home of the old Indian who adopted Cole, Powaw.

To his disappointment, when he arrives at Powaw's house, it seems empty too.

Cole's relatives may just happen to be out. But Angel has doubts. He looked into Cole. After some digging, Angel learned Cole is no safety inspector. The former Delta Force commando could've expected a maneuver against his relatives and sent them away.

According to Wayne, Cole's been on the lam ever since his supposed killing of Earl Laughlin. Meaning he never had the time to clear his home of possessions that could be exploited.

Angel drives to Cole's cabin. He locates the window Earl broke and climbs inside. Bullet marks on the refrigerator and cabinet. In the den, a shattered table, a trace of Pine-Sol in the air.

He opens the laptop on the desk. A password is required, but he still takes the computer. He can remove the hard drive to access its data.

He looks around for anything else of interest. An object on the floor catches his attention.

A Polaroid picture. He picks it up. The image appears recent. Cole sits at a dining table next to a pretty, dark-haired woman in her late twenties. Both are smiling.

And now, so is Angel.

31

Cole hikes through the wilderness over steep, dense terrain. The radio he stole from the cop is clipped to his waist. He's listened to police chatter, overhearing where officers were sent in the woods to look for him. He went elsewhere.

His goal is to keep evading them until the DEA arrives. Agent Ramirez could demand the cops stand down and escort Cole to safety. But hiding out here that long will be far from easy. A chopper search should soon start.

The aching from Cole's rib and bullet wound worsens with the strenuous physicality. His boots struggle to negotiate a rock face slick with rainwater.

His burner vibrates. *Lacey.* "Hey," he says into the phone.

"What's up?"

"Oh, nothing much." With the phone tucked between his ear and shoulder, he grips a boulder with both hands and swings his feet onto a ledge. "How'd you get this number?"

"Your other one wasn't working. I found your sister-in-law on Instagram and asked her if she saw you. She told me to call you on this. I know that might sound a little paranoid, but I saw something. And I just had to tell you."

His jaw clenches. "Yeah?"

"So I'm in my kitchen making coffee and noticed something through the window kinda weird. At your place."

"Okay."

"Yesterday, when you said those gunshots were just from hunters, I didn't think much of it. Then later I saw a cop car stop by."

"The cop thing was unconnected. Just a few questions they wanted me to answer about my brother's case." He feels bad lying to her, but doesn't want to worry her.

"Well, all right. Then today, minutes ago, I see a car, not your Jeep, pull into your driveway. I was first like, Cole must've taken an Uber home or something. But when the guy got out, it wasn't you."

"What guy?"

"So you weren't expecting anyone at your house this morning?"

"What did he look like?"

"Black hair, ponytail. Big, bigger than you. I thought maybe he was a friend of yours. But then he climbed in through a window. Between the gunshots, the cops, then that, I started to get nervous. Thought I should call you."

Cole doesn't recall any guy like that from the Freedom Riders photos. He doesn't suspect Lacey saw a dirty cop either. Policemen in Timber Ridge tend to have crewcuts, not ponytails. This man is something new. He may be the worse problem Sandra warned about.

"Is he still in my cabin?" Cole asks.

"He just left."

She said he pulled up minutes ago. If he left so soon, he might've already found something of value. Cole closes his eyes and imagines the objects in his cabin.

An icy sensation runs through him.

The Polaroid.

The Freedom Riders and police had no clue about Cole's connection to Lacey. No pictures exist on the internet of them together. They've never even done a social activity in public. He didn't have to worry about her as a target. Until now.

Attempting to keep his voice calm, he says, "Lacey, I'm going to need you to get in your car and drive away from your house."

"What?"

"No need to panic. Just—"

"You think this guy is going to break into my place next or something?"

"Please, just get in your—"

"I have a shift. I'm about to go in."

"You can't go to the diner. He could be waiting for you there." Cole realizes how jarring this must sound to her, but now that she's in danger, he owes her direct honesty.

"Oh God," she says. "This man is coming after me specifically? Who is he? What does he want?"

"Spend the night at a friend's house outside Timber—"

"I'm not with Declan. He's at school. I can't just abandon him for the night."

If this man knew Lacey happened to live next to Cole, he would've already grabbed her. But address information isn't hard to find.

"Just leave your house and take a drive," Cole says.

"I'm calling the cops."

"Don't."

"I'm not safe. I'm bugging out. I'm calling the cops."

"You have to trust me on this. Drive down to me. I'll keep you safe until this is all over. I actually can use a ride. We can help each other out."

"Down to where?"

"The woods in Danesville. I'll drop you a pin."

"What the heck are you doing in the woods in Danesville?"

"I'll explain when you get here. Check your mirrors for any cars that might linger behind you on the road. If you notice something like that, call me."

"This is a real...butt-flavored bowl of cereal. Okay. See you soon." She hangs up.

32

A ngel carries his unopened umbrella at his side, rain tapping his wide-brimmed hat. He is used to the flatness of Texas. This is his first time in Montana, the first he's seen high peaks outside Afghanistan. He snaps a photo of the valley surrounding the public park and adds it to an album he created on his phone titled *Splendors of Montana.*

Wayne sits on a bench with an open umbrella. His attention is on the empty playground bordered with wildflowers dying in the mid-October chill.

Angel sits beside him. Wayne, wearing a cowboy hat, turns to him and says, "Hi again."

Angel passes him the Polaroid. "The woman. Who is she?"

Wayne's nostrils flare. His eyes widen. He is hushed for a few seconds. "I...uh, sorry...I don't know."

Angel analyzes his expression. He doesn't believe him.

"What is she, Cole's girlfriend or something?" Wayne asks.

"Ugly truths may be difficult to grasp in a town as scenic as this. In the grass among these beautiful flowers, insects are murdering each other. In the woods, animals doing the same. No different with humans. Food, territory, possessions. Only achieved through competition. Winners and losers. What a delightfully twisted sense of humor God must have watching all his children slaughter each other for the limited resources he bestowed. Here I feel obliged to remind you of your debt to Ernesto."

A slight shudder to Wayne's shoulders. "I'm here to help you. But I don't know the woman. Really."

Angel peers into his eyes. "I like you, Wayne. Especially that nifty outfit of yours. I feel like I'm looking at a chic, silver-fox version of the Marlboro Man."

"Uh. Thank…thank you."

"But if I find out you're lying to me, I might not like you anymore."

Wayne takes a deep breath and nods. They watch the playground swings, a slight sway to them in the wind.

Wayne points at the towering pine trees around them. "Years ago, Timber Ridge was just wilderness. My great-grandpa changed that. He went to a poker game one Saturday night in Bozeman. He was no more than eighteen. Wagered money he didn't even have, on credit, and won. Bought a tractor. Cleared enough trees to make a road, sold the farmland. And kept going from there, clearing and selling."

Angel says nothing.

"The country was a different place back then," Wayne says. "Still a frontier. So much room to grow. Those old-timers had it a lot easier than us."

"I disagree. A frontier is still out there. The mentality now… that's the difference. Most men today are tame. They're brainwashed by schools and the media to be weak, convinced it's a virtue called civility. The men who actually run this country, though, the ones who dictate what the schools teach and the media broadcasts, I've worked for some of them. Nothing tame about them. How about you, Wayne? Would you say you're a civil man?"

Wayne opens his mouth. Then closes it, as if hesitating on his answer. Angel gives him a firm pat on the upper thigh and walks back to his car.

Before coming to the park, Angel combed through Cole's followers on Instagram and friends on Facebook to see if any profile pictures matched the woman in the Polaroid. No luck. They could be in the early stage of dating. Couples tend not to connect in public on social media until a relationship is official.

Angel noticed Cole belonged to a Facebook group for graduates of Timber Ridge High. If the woman in the Polaroid is from town, she could belong to one too. Guessing she's twenty-seven, he locates the alumni group for that year and scrolls through the member photos. No. He tries the group from the year before. No again. But another year back, a picture seems to match.

He visits her profile. Her current city is Timber Ridge. He flips through more of her photos, assessing her face from a few angles.

Lacey Carter it is.

33

Lacey coasts to a stop in her white Volkswagen on the side of a road in Danesville. She wears a leather jacket over a V-neck tee shirt. A knock on her passenger window startles her.

Cole waves and climbs in. "I'll pay you back for this," he says, pointing at the new sweatshirt and hair dye on the passenger seat. He texted her about buying them.

"Yeah, hi," she says.

He slips the dark-gray Carhartt sweatshirt over his torn flannel and lifts the hood over his head. He points at the road. "Keep going the way you came."

She leans on the gas. "My friend from the diner called me after I left Walmart. Your picture is apparently all over channel eight. For killing a cop. Please tell me it wasn't really you."

"It was me."

She hits the brake. Not in a seatbelt, he falls forward.

She pulls onto the shoulder. "You tricked me to come out here so I could be, what, a fugitive getaway driver?" She balls her fists, taps them against her face. "I can't do this. Get out. Please just get out."

He sits back up in the seat. He lifts his sweatshirt and flannel and pulls down a bandage, revealing a gunshot wound. "The cop did this to me first."

She grimaces.

"It was self-defense," he says. "The guy was crooked. Bad people are after me. Unfortunately, they're after you too. You can't be alone."

She stares into his eyes for a moment, then sighs. Yes, she's mad at him. But she does believe him.

"Just...I want...just tell me what I need to do to be safe," she says.

"If the operator you saw at my house is any good, it won't be long till he gets into a DMV database to see what you drive, and other crooked cops put out a BOLO for it. We need to get out of the area, find an anonymous place without external visibility, and hang there for a few hours till reinforcements arrive. If we're somehow found before then, I'll...see what I can do."

She's quiet for a moment. "I thought you were a safety inspector."

He looks away. "I spent some time in the army."

The car is silent besides some voice coming out of a radio on his waist.

She lets out a long exhale and cruises back onto the road. "So we're hiding from the weirdo who broke into your house, plus corrupt cops?"

"In full disclosure, also a biker gang."

"Sure. Let's toss that on the list too."

"It's a lot, I know. But we'll get through it."

"Ugh. God, okay. So where should I drive, like a motel?"

"I considered that. But they'll make us put down a credit card and ID. The cops will be checking occupancy lists."

She holds up her index finger. "Not all motels require a credit card and ID. Got cash on you?"

"Not much, but I don't think you're right about—"

"You're not the only one who's found themself in questionable circumstances before. I have some experience keeping a low profile too."

"Little did I know I was in the presence of a hardened G."

"Nothing illegal. I was just…a bit more adventurous when I was younger. One of those adventures happened to involve a motel room. Let's leave it at that."

"Left."

"Look up places. No national chains. They have to follow all sorts of rules. Mom and pops. If possible, sleazy."

He smirks. "Sleazy, huh?"

She gives him a playful glare.

In her rearview mirror, a helicopter circles a mountaintop a few miles behind them, a police search. The playfulness leaves her expression. The harsh reality of their situation hits her.

He shows her a photo on his phone of a single-story building, weeds sprouting near the base of a signpost that says *Paradise Inn*. She nods.

On the trip there, she asks him a slew of questions about what on earth is going on. He answers all of them, addressing his brother's predatory loan from guys called the Freedom Riders, a confrontation at The Knotted Vine, his seizure of millions of dollars of opioids, the DEA, some mysterious guy called Gator, a local police sergeant's betrayal, and the bad people's incentive to harm those close to Cole.

"I feel horrible getting you wrapped up in this," he says.

"Let's just make sure we get unwrapped from it."

After hearing his story, her anger at him wanes. He was just trying to protect his family. Yet her anxiety increases. He, and she, face much severer problems than an arrest.

They drive for another fifteen minutes or so while she explains her motel plan. They exit into a town called Grinson, a bit bigger than Danesville. Run-down mobile homes scatter a swath of land, an old wooden windmill spinning.

"There's a deli like a mile from here," he says, looking at his phone. "They should have an ATM. The cops might already have access to my debit-card transactions. Mind using yours? I'll pay you back as soon as this is all over."

She nods.

"Your car," he says. "Let's hide it in the woods so the chopper doesn't spot it."

She pulls between a gap in the trees and rolls through the foliage. She gets out with her pink umbrella, he the hair dye.

They walk through the forest. Soon a little downtown emerges. A post office, a New Age church, a liquor store, other shops. She takes out money from the deli's ATM and they go about another mile toward the Paradise Inn. To avoid a security camera, Cole waits in the woods while she enters the office.

A cow skull hangs on the wall. A tall, beefy clerk in his mid-twenties, in a tee shirt and suspenders, hunches over the counter, fixated on his phone, video game noises coming out of it.

"One second," he says without lifting his eyes. "Just got to torch one more bad guy." His thick thumbs hit the screen. He laughs. "Burn, you dingus." A theme song blares. He silences it, then looks up at Lacey. He blinks a few times as if surprised to see a pretty woman in this dump. "How can I help you, miss?"

"Hi. I need a room."

"How many nights?"

"None. Just a few hours."

"We only do nights."

"Okay. One."

"Weekdays are forty-nine bucks."

"Sure."

"Credit card and ID."

She leans toward him with a smile. "When a woman asks to

check into a motel for just a few hours, do you think she's up to anything she wants made public?"

"Do whatever you want in there. I'm not going to tell anyone. I still need a credit card and ID, though."

"I'm married."

"Honeymoon? Congrats."

"I'm meeting a man here who is not my husband."

"Ah."

"Divorce attorneys hire pesky PIs who go through financial records to expose infidelity. So, as you can imagine, I'd prefer not to put down a credit card."

"Well, the boss says I still need one. In case you, like, wreck something."

"Totally understand. What's the most expensive thing in the room?"

"I dunno."

"The TV?"

"I guess."

"What's a good TV go for these days, about three hundred?" She opens her purse, sets a wad of cash on the counter. "Here's four. Forty-nine for the room. Hold onto three hundred until I leave, for the TV. As for the rest, that's for you to keep if you let this slide."

He counts the money. And nods. He hands her a numbered piece of yellow plastic, a metal key attached with a rubber band.

"Thank you so much," she says. "Also, cool suspenders. Very punk."

He smiles. She texts Cole: *Room 5.*

34

Angel exits a highway and coasts onto a street hollowed with potholes. He drives by a trailer park with hideous mobile homes and a decrepit windmill. Yet the trees and mountains behind are majestic. He snaps a photo for his album, careful not to include any unpleasant-looking human creation in the frame. He cruises for a few minutes toward a strip of businesses. A yellow-and-black sign rises from the horizon.

Paradise Inn.

He parks in the lot. He does not see a white Volkswagen, the vehicle Lacey Carter drives. Yet he is still confident she's here.

He gave her name to Sergeant Sandra Evans, who pulled a file on her from the police database. Once he had Lacey's phone number, he performed a successful tracking tactic. She is in a motel room. He is just uncertain which.

Sandra asked him if she should send police units to bring Lacey to the station for questioning. Angel said his questioning style would be more effective.

From a Home Depot shopping bag, he grabs his new gloves and puts them on. He slips the roll of duct tape into a pocket of his duster, grabs his modified umbrella, and steps out of the Toyota.

He tugs his big-brimmed hat low, a shield from security cameras, and enters the motel's office.

The husky clerk is transfixed on some sort of game on his phone. Angel approaches the counter and says, "Hi there."

"One second." The guy's thumbs hit his screen. "So...need a room?"

"You play that game often?"

"You're into it too?"

"No. Just curious."

"Yeah, I play kinda a lot."

"What do you get if you beat the game?"

"Umm. It's just...you don't get money or anything, if that's what you're asking. It's just a normal game."

"Hmm."

"You want a room or not, man?"

"I do not." Angel shows him a Timber Ridge police badge obtained from Sandra. "I'm looking for someone I believe checked in here sometime today."

"A criminal?"

"A dangerous one."

"What does he look like?"

"Not a he." Angel shows him a photo he screenshotted from Lacey's Facebook profile.

"That chick? What the hell did she do?"

"Drowned her nephew. We found the body this morning. Now she's on the run."

"Holy shit." The clerk lifts his palm to his forehead. "How do you know it was her?"

"I am not at liberty to divulge details of an ongoing investigation. All I need is her room number."

The clerk sets his hands on the counter. He eyes Angel's outfit. "You know…you don't really look like a cop."

"I'm a plain-clothes detective."

The clerk smirks. "I got to say, that was pretty good. You may've fooled someone else, but not me. Nah-ah. You work for that woman's husband's lawyer. Hoping to take a picture through her window, catch her in the act."

Excellent news. She's here with a man, could be Cole. "You have a vivid imagination," Angel says. "Maybe from spending so much time in all those fake worlds on your telephone."

"Look, I've got a cousin who's a sheriff's deputy. I'll call him over. He can let me know if you're a real cop…or just some jackoff with a fake badge who makes a living perving on nice ladies." The clerk taps his phone screen.

Angel sets four fingers on the back of his hand. "Do not do that."

"What? This is America. I can do whatever I want."

"No you can't."

Fear trickles into the clerk's expression. "Who are you for real?"

"A man who is giving you one more chance to do what he is asking."

Silence for a few seconds.

"Yeah," the clerk says. "Whatever, fine. Let me check the visitor book for her room number."

Angel smiles.

The clerk bends as if searching for something in a cubby. When he rises, a Louisville Slugger bat is in his grip.

He swings it at Angel. Who ducks and bashes the wrench umbrella down on the clerk's left shoulder joint, then right, the impact to the coracohumeral ligaments stunning his arms. The guy drops the bat.

Angel climbs onto the counter, the duster flaring around him.

The clerk throws a right hook with his weakened arm. Angel hops over the punch and lands on the other side of the desk, where the clerk scrambles for the Louisville Slugger rolling across the floor.

With the umbrella, Angel backhands the clerk's outer left knee, collapsing him. Angel pushes the bat across the room with the heel of his boot, well out of the clerk's reach, then strolls to the window and flips off the neon *Vacancy* sign.

He closes the blinds, locks the door, and paces back to the guy, who's crawled to a desk drawer and is rooting through it.

Holding a pair of scissors, the clerk rises to his feet, his balance unsteady on a damaged knee. He limps to Angel and slashes at him. Smirking, Angel avoids the attack with a casual sidestep, then sweeps his ankle, crashing him to the floor.

Angel presses a boot on the clerk's wrist and rips the scissors from his hand. Angel's smirk widens. He positions a blade tip on the clerk's eye and slices his cornea.

35

The gloomy daylight squeezes through the closed blinds in room 5 of the Paradise Inn. A watercolor painting of a cowboy riding a bronco hangs on the wall. In the bathroom, Cole dyed his hair dark brown, wrung out his rain-wet clothes, and dried off before putting them back on. Some warmth has returned to his skin.

"It's called two truths and a lie," Lacey says, sitting at a small laminate table, its rim peeling. Cole propped its second chair against the door, an added barrier to the lock in case someone tries to bust in. Now that they're in a secure place, Lacey's nerves seem to have calmed a bit.

"How do you win?" Cole asks. He stands by the queen bed, removing a screw from the headboard, using a dime from Lacey's purse as a screwdriver.

"It's a game," she says. "But not like a competition. Just a fun way to pass the time. You say three things. Two real, one BS. The other person has to guess the fake one."

"I can handle that."

"I'll go first." She brushes a strand of her straight, dark hair from her face. "I once won five hundred bucks on a scratch-off lottery ticket. I know how to play the saxophone. I've never eaten cauliflower."

"You can't play a lick on the sax."

"How the heck did you get that so quick?"

He removes an aluminum post about a foot long from the headboard. "It's psychological. The point of the game is to guard the lie. People feel vulnerable when something they want to defend is in an outside position. You said the sax thing second, in the middle of your two truths. You were protecting it."

"Not fair." She puts on an exaggerated pout like she's mad at him, while her gaze suggests she's impressed.

"So what's your gripe with cauliflower?"

"Always thought it looked like little brains. Like they got it from the heads of mice."

He grins. "Thanks for ruining it for me now. I'll be staying away from cauliflower, not to mention butt-flavored cereal."

She laughs. "I was nervous, that just sorta came out." Those long-lashed blue eyes of hers survey him. "You learn that psychological stuff in the army?"

He nods while securing the headboard post in his jeans. It'd make for a decent weapon.

"I doubt they teach all that to regular soldiers," she says. "You were involved in more serious things, huh?"

He's lied about this to so many people for so long. But he's put her through a lot today. She deserves the truth. "I guess you could say that," he says.

"Jeez. What motivated you to get into all that?"

"I suppose it was losing my parents. Just a year later, when I was a freshman, Nine Eleven happened. So many kids were forced to go through what I did. I decided my time would best be spent trying to prevent an attack like that from happening again."

She is silent and still for a couple seconds, thin bars of daylight from the blinds striping her face. Then she slants her head and nods as if she both understands his answer and appreciates it.

"What's happening now with fentanyl in Timber Ridge is worse in a way," he says. "On Nine Eleven, a lot of kids lost their parents. But with these drug ODs, parents are losing their kids. I've never experienced that, but imagine it's even harder."

"Me too."

Her phone, on the table, rings. She answers. "Hey Brooke… Yes. Thank you so much for scooping him up from school…Then if he can hang out at your house and play with Liam for a few hours, that would be lovely…He'll eat just about anything…Yeah, I'm fine. Just got pulled into a personal thing. We'll be sure to have Liam over next week…Thanks again. Yep, bye." She hangs up, taps her text message icon, and scrolls to a conversation with *Declan*.

"Wait," Cole says, nodding at her screen. "What's that?"

She gives him a confused look.

He points at a text in her inbox, its timestamp about an hour ago: *Thanks. We won't send you any stock tips.*

"It's just some marketing junk I got," she says.

"Open it up."

She taps the message, revealing an earlier one: *Would you like to receive free stock tips? Press yes or no.*

"You hitting that no link could've been an issue," he says.

"What issue?"

"A tech on my team did something like this once on an op."

"Sent out spam about the stock market?"

"Weight-loss pills. Same goal though. We were in Honduras trying to find a man we needed to…deal with. The tech sent him a text that looked like mass spam, with yes and no options. Even though the guy chose no, he still hit a link, which made his phone pass info back to an army server. The tech used that to track the phone's location."

The rosiness in her cheeks vanishes. "I had no clue that was even a thing."

"Not your fault. Shut it off."

He texts Powaw and Melanie, warning them not to respond to any marketing messages they may receive, and if they already did, to separate from their phones now.

Cole nudges the blinds aside and assesses the surrounding area. He spots a car in the lot he does not remember from earlier. A silver Toyota. He points at it and turns to Lacey.

"Shit," she says, leaning over his shoulder, peeking out the window. "That's the one I saw at your house."

Cole closes the blinds. "I want you to stay calm."

"Okay," she says, her voice not calm.

"Put the phone on the bed. Even if it's off, it can still possibly be tracked."

She flings it on the mattress.

"GPS is accurate at an address level, but not a room one," he says. "He knows we're at the motel, but not exactly where in the motel." He grabs her purse from the dresser and hands it to her, then puts up his hood. "We need to leave without him noticing." He points at the bathroom. "We get to your car and get out of town."

"I thought you said being in my car before the DEA got here was bad."

"This guy running up on us with a gun would be a worse kind of bad."

"Ugh." She slaps her thighs. "Okay, okay." She closes her eyes, takes a deep breath, and opens them.

"I won't leave your side. Come on." He leads her into the

bathroom and opens its window. She steps up onto the closed toilet lid, then crawls out of the one-story building onto long, unmanicured grass. He does the same and closes the window behind them.

He looks around. Nobody is watching. They jog in the direction of her Volkswagen two miles away.

36

Angel paces the Paradise Inn's storage room with the wrench umbrella. Shelves of cream-colored sheets and towels surround him, standing against cinderblock walls without windows. He stares at the clerk, whose neck is duct-taped to a floor-to-ceiling drainpipe, his wrists bound behind his back.

Tears flow down his cheeks. His scissor-cut left eyeball, discolored and swollen, twitches. Angel was careful to only lacerate his cornea, a rare part of the body that does not bleed, none of the man's blood on the office carpet. The clerk struggles against the duct-tape restraints without success. His crying loudens.

"Was it the rough play in the office that has you weeping?" Angel asks. "I caught a glimpse of that video game of yours. Lighting people on fire, quite graphic. Much worse than what I did to you. That may be about to change though." Angel unbuttons the clerk's jeans.

"What...what're you doing?"

Whistling, Angel unsnaps the guy's suspenders, unzips his fly, and lowers his pants to mid-thigh, revealing red boxers. "How many inches is it?"

"Huh?"

"Oh, come on. Don't be shy. You've definitely measured." He whispers, "We all have."

"Help," the clerk screams.

Angel slaps his hand over his mouth, muffling him. "If you continue yelling, I'm going to take off two inches with the scissors. If you keep your voice down, but still refuse to tell me that woman's room number, I'll take off just one. If you keep your voice down and give me the room number, I'll take off nothing. You have my word."

The clerk's sweaty head nods, his good eye consumed with panic.

Angel removes his hand from his mouth.

"Five," the guy says in a trembly voice. "Room five."

"Thank you. Now give me the password for the computer at the front desk and I'll let you go."

"Bingo seventy-seven. All lowercase."

Angel backhands him across the temple with the wrench umbrella, the force popping his good eyeball a few millimeters out from the skull. His head jerks to his shoulder. Angel cracks his other temple, the head thrashing the other way, then bangs it with another backhand.

The tip of the clerk's tongue protrudes from his mouth. No movement to his face. Dead.

Angel exits the storage room into the office, unlocks the desktop computer, and searches for a surveillance program. He finds something called Vortex Security. He locates the file for today's camera recording and tries to delete it. But the system admin disabled erasing on this account.

Though Angel's hat hid most of his face, the video could still present a problem. If so, he'll handle it.

For now, his focus is Lacey and Cole. Angel finds a spare key marked 5 and steps outside into the brisk mountain air.

With his hand on the silencer-equipped 9mm at his waist, he unlocks 5's door, shoots the legs off the chair blocking it, and enters an empty room. A pink umbrella in the corner. A phone on the bed.

He checks the closet. Nobody inside. The shower, nobody either. But on the toilet lid, a bit of dirt. Maybe from a shoe. He climbs onto the lid and slinks out the window. The overgrown grass is flattened as if just stepped on. The trail points east.

37

C ole doesn't jog through the woods to the Volkswagen as fast as he'd like. He lost a lot of blood last night, didn't sleep, only ate a few chunks of bagel this morning, and twisted his ankle running from the cops.

"You may not have intended to drag me into this ordeal," Lacey says, sounding winded, "but you still seriously owe me."

"Can't argue with that."

"Dinner at your house tomorrow night. Lobsters. And the expensive fish-egg stuff."

"Caviar."

"Plenty of that. Plus champagne."

"Maybe I'll hire a guy to stand in the corner and play a violin."

"Him. Also an electrical massage thing to rub my feet, which are going to be crazy sore."

"Noted."

His ears pick up an engine on the road behind them. He peeks over his shoulder, through the trees. The Toyota moves east. "He's coming. Don't panic."

"You saying that, Cole, automatically makes me panic."

Cole hides with her behind a pine. He debates continuing to her car. But this guy could be looking for the make and model on the road. They'd be better off finding a new indoor place to lie low in town.

Cole waits for the Toyota to pass, then says, "This way." He goes down a hill out of the brush and into an alley in Grinson's small business district.

He looks at the backs of nearby buildings. One's rear door is propped open. The New Age church, on the door *The Ministry of Light* beside a star logo.

He turns off his police radio to eliminate its noise and peeks inside. Nobody is in the back room. He sidles through the doorway, Lacey following, into a shadowy area jumbled with cardboard boxes. A purple curtain hangs ahead.

A male voice on the other side, in the tone of a preacher, says, "Peace is always the answer, brothers and sisters." Applause from a crowd. "If someone insults you, do not insult back. If someone hits you, do not hit back. Yes, this world can be dark. But it is up to us to be the light."

Cole kicks out the wooden wedge propping the rear door and closes it behind them. He waves her to the curtain. His footfalls are slow and quiet, she mimicking. He moves the fabric a couple inches aside and notes exit routes, lines of sight, and possible obstacles in the bigger room.

A skinny middle-aged man in a green leisure suit paces a stage, about a dozen men and women in chintzy clothing facing him on wooden benches. On the wall is a ten-foot mural of Jesus in a tee shirt and jeans with stars radiating from his head.

In about twenty minutes, the front door opens and the preacher stops talking. A man stands in the entryway, casting a long shadow on the aisle between the benches.

Lacey squeezes Cole's arm as if to signal this is the guy she saw earlier. All-black clothing, an umbrella hanging off his wrist.

The wide-brimmed booney hat helps hide his face, the gloves a shield against fingerprints.

The church congregation eyeballs him.

"Can I help you, young man?" the preacher asks.

"I apologize for interrupting." He flashes a badge. "I'm a detective. A fugitive was reported in the area. I doubt anybody here is in danger. I just want to do a quick check of the property for any traces."

He could've anticipated Cole's decision to hide somewhere indoors and is checking the handful of downtown businesses.

"Oh my," the preacher says. "Yes, please." He steps away from the podium with an antsy expression.

The man in all black opens a confession booth and peers inside.

Cole takes Lacey's hand in his and scoots to the rear door. He pushes on it.

Cluduck, a metallic thud. It doesn't open. He tries again. *Cluduck*.

"What's wrong?" she whispers.

"He must've tried this door first," Cole whispers back. "When he couldn't get in, he put the wooden wedge on the other side in case we were here. So we couldn't get out."

She clenches her teeth. "How the heck do we leave, then?"

He looks around for a window back here. None. Above them, though, is a grid of fiberboard tiles known as a drop ceiling. On the other side would be an upper space a couple feet high with cables, pipes, and ventilation ducts.

He jumps and taps a tile out of place, careful to keep his noise low. He jumps again and clasps the metal gridwork. The thin strips in his hands shake a bit. Before they break, he reaches up and clutches a cast-iron pipe with a solid horizontal mount.

He lifts his legs into the upper space and wraps his feet around the pipe.

"Your purse," he whispers down to Lacey. "Stuff it in your jacket."

She crams it in the front of her leather coat, preventing dangling. He lowers his arm to her. She climbs it, but struggles to get all the way up to the pipe.

Footsteps approach. Dread spreads on Lacey's face.

Cole lifts her higher. She grabs the pipe. He scoops his arm under her legs and hoists the rest of her into the upper space.

He slides down on the pipe, making room for her feet to wrap it, then nudges the fiberboard tile back in place.

The footsteps louden as if now in the back room. *Dutt.* A second. *Dutt, dutt.* Five seconds. *Dutt, dutt, dutt.*

Lacey's legs quiver as she struggles to hang onto the pipe.

Dutt, dutt.

One of her feet slips off.

Cole shoots out one of his feet, catching her shoe before it clunks the fiberboard. He takes a deep breath.

He guides her sneaker back to the pipe, helps her re-interlock her feet, and presses his ankle on them to prevent another slip.

Dutt, dutt, the sounds softer now as if the man in all black is returning to the front of the church.

In a few seconds the preacher asks, "Find anything?"

"No. But I hope to soon." The church's front door slams shut.

38

Angel exits a barbershop a few doors down from The Ministry of Light church. He just pulled his detective routine in the last of Grinson's downtown buildings. No sign of Cole and Lacey in any.

Angel pulls a cigarillo out of a pack from his pocket and sparks it, cupping his hand to block the drizzle. He sucks in a drag and blows out smoke. Two sixtyish White ladies leaving the post office glimpse him from under their umbrellas.

He smokes, thinks. He rolls up his sleeve, exposing a few inches of skin, and flicks some hot ash on the underside of his wrist. Dots of pain crackle through his flesh.

The first time hot ash was sprinkled on him was in Mexico at age seven, a trip his father took him on to visit his paternal grandfather. The old man was not nice to young Angel. When his dad went to the bathroom, his granddad tapped his cigarillo on the edge of the table near the boy's hand, bits of ember burning the back. It was no accident. Not till years later did Angel understand this hostility directed at him. The traditional Mexican elder did not approve of his son's White wife and, by extension, their half-White boy. Angel was considered inferior.

Once a Navy SEAL, while the enemy closed in on him, he'd singe himself with a cigarillo as a reminder of the pain of feeling inferior.

He calls the leader of the Freedom Riders.

"Who's this?" Russell asks.

"Gator's new friend from Texas."

"Ah. I've heard good things about you. Me and my boys are ready to help. What's the deal?"

"I'm in a remote part of the county. Cole and the woman are here. I'm unsure where in particular though."

"Want me to send a couple swinging dicks over to help you look?"

"There was a complication at a motel. I need to leave before someone stumbles on the byproduct. While I'm on the road, I need one of your men to pursue a strategy up in Timber Ridge."

"Hit me."

"If executed properly, this tactic works well. It can bring Cole right to us. But only a man with a stomach for the unpleasant can pull it off."

Russell is silent for a few seconds.

"Russell?" Angel says. "Is that going to be a problem?"

"Uh, no. We...we're here for you."

Angel explains what needs to be done, ends the call, and walks to his car.

"Excuse me?" a guy says behind him.

A county cop.

"Yes?" Angel asks.

"My pal at the liquor store said you were in town poking around. Is this about the fugitive from Timber Ridge? Maddox?"

"Exactly."

"I didn't hear anything come over the radio about him being in Grinson."

"Nothing is confirmed yet. I'm just investigating a comment by a friend of a friend."

"Who said what?"

Just before Angel gives a fake answer, a voice from the cop's radio says, "All available units, possible one eight seven at Paradise Inn."

187. The police code for murder.

The cop's posture straightens. "Be right there," he says into the radio, then looks at Angel. "This Maddox guy may've just killed someone else. Let's go. You can ride with me."

Angel can't go back there. The officers at the crime scene are sure to get a copy of the surveillance footage from the motel owner.

The cop waves at his car. It's pulled over in an alley across the street. Though a few pedestrians are on the sidewalks, none have visibility into the alley.

Angel jogs alongside the cop to the cruiser.

The cop opens the driver's door. Angel snaps his neck. His body plops to the asphalt. Reaching into the car, Angel pops the trunk, then loads the corpse into it and closes the hatch.

Angel hears a thump behind him. He looks over his shoulder. A grocery bag lies on the pavement, an orange rolling about. A man in a red jacket stares with an open mouth. He must've just left the deli, noticed Angel hiding the dead cop, and dropped his bag in shock.

The witness runs along the sidewalk, out of view from the alley. Angel chases him. If this guy calls 9-1-1, some of those available units heading to the motel will split off to the deli, no more than a mile away.

Angel hears an engine. The witness pulls onto the town's main road in a Silverado pickup. Angel sprints after it. His strides are long, powerful, and fast, like an NFL wide receiver's. He jumps at the truck. His hands latch onto the top of the tailgate.

The truck speeds up. Angel dives into the bed.

The witness takes his phone out of his jacket. Angel bangs his umbrella against the rear windshield. It cracks.

The startled witness puts down the phone, returns both hands to the wheel, and yanks it left, then right, then left, as if trying to toss Angel out of the truck.

Angel presses his stomach on the bed and extends his legs to its sides, his low center of gravity keeping him stabilized.

The witness turns onto an upward-sloping street. Angel jostles a bit.

The truck ticks up to about sixty miles per hour. Angel thwacks the windshield again, deepening the crack. To his left is a massive rock face, to his right a steep cliff without a guardrail.

While the truck rides the S-shaped road, Angel smacks the glass again, busting a hole in it, shards flying into the backseat. The sound of a country song flows outside.

The witness swerves, kicking the truck's rear toward the cliff. Angel loses his footing. His shoulder nails the bed's wall, but he remains in. He backhands the windshield. The hole widens to about two feet. He clobbers it again, then again.

His heavy coat shields his torso from the hole's jagged rim as he slips into the truck's cabin.

The witness fumbles for his phone in the cupholder.

Angel maneuvers his legs through the windshield. Glass slivers on the backseat crunch beneath his boots.

The witness taps his screen. With just one hand on the wheel, he loses control on the windy road. Before he can finish dialing, Angel bats the phone out of his hand with the umbrella.

The Silverado zips about eighty MPH along the cliff, a tire sliding off the asphalt. The truck almost falls over the edge.

Angel clamps his hands over the witness's eyes.

The man tries to pull them off, but isn't strong enough. He veers into the opposite lane. A ragtop convertible weaves around them, horn honking. The side of the truck grates against the rock face. Sparks shoot.

"Fuck," the witness grumbles.

"If you don't pull over, we're both going to die."

Another honking car swerves around them, its nose clipping a truck headlight. The cabin shakes.

"This isn't working," Angel says.

"Fine, shit." The witness eases off the gas. The truck stops on a diagonal, blocking a lane and a half.

Angel keeps his hands over the man's eyes. The witness grasps his keys. Something metallic punctures the back of Angel's gloved hand.

He glances at it. A Swiss Army knife is attached to the keychain. A small blade protrudes from his flesh, drawing blood.

Angel frees himself from the knife and winds up with the umbrella to hammer the witness's head. Before he can, the man lunges at him. He juts his blade at Angel's throat.

Angel dodges it. It slices the shoulder of his jacket. He clutches the back of the man's head. And forces his face toward the spiky bottom edge of the windshield hole.

The man presses his hands against the backseat. His neck strains trying to keep his face above the glass.

Angel maneuvers behind him. He grasps the man's head with both hands and pushes harder.

The man's necklace dangles. Its crucifix taps the glass. Angel aims the man's eyeball at a long, thin shard.

The strength in the guy's neck withers. "Please, no. Not like this."

Angel lowers his eyeball onto the tip of the glass spike. He screams. Angel applies more pressure. The witness's head lowers. Blood squirts onto the leather seat. The screaming intensifies.

More blood splatters. The man's elbows go slack. His face drops farther, the rest of the spike vanishing inside him.

Angel removes his hands from the man's sweaty head. He catches his breath, staring at the slumped-over corpse, then lifts it off the glass, revealing an eyeball severed in half and a socket welled with blood.

He removes his jacket and the witness's. He ties the black one around the man's face, containing the bleeding, puts on the red North Face, and takes off the booney hat. The new coat and lack of hat should help alter his appearance from the motel's surveillance video.

He opens the door and drags the dead body across the pavement. He kicks it over the cliff. It tumbles against outcroppings and settles in a cluster of overgrown bushes. Angel climbs behind the truck's wheel and drives down the mountain toward his Toyota.

39

The youngest Freedom Rider, twenty-two-year-old Bridger Sparks, lurks behind a tree at Timber Ridge Middle School. Before he came here, he snorted a mound of cocaine to amp himself up, his pulse pounding, sweat trickling down his forehead.

Bridger is honored he was tasked with this important job. A runaway from Arizona, he met Russell at sixteen while working as an apprentice tattoo artist. Russell, who liked a tat he did for him, was the first person to tell Bridger he had talent. Soon other Freedom Riders came to him for their ink and, within a couple years, Bridger was admitted into the gang.

His burner phone vibrates. A text message from Sergeant Sandra: *Now*. Russell forced her to play a part in the plan. Her job was to get inside, distract the security guard, and prop open a side door.

Bridger cracks his knuckles and neck and paces through the door. Class in session, the halls are empty. He removed his hoop earring. He wears a baggy tan jumpsuit Sandra got him, the uniform of school janitors in Timber Ridge. Its long sleeves cover his tattoos. He takes a cleaning rag out of his pocket.

Sandra, who has access to all Timber Ridge municipal documents, was also instructed to send a PDF of the school's map to him, plus the schedule of a sixth-grade student.

Declan Carter.

She at first protested. Russell threatened to not just kill her, but her mother. Sandra's been making a lot of dough under the table off the Freedom Riders' hard work. Dirty money comes with dirty obligations. She has no business complaining about the life she chose.

In four minutes, Declan should be getting out of science class and making his way to math in 31A.

Bridger turns a corner. He kneels near 31A with his face to the wall, pretending to wipe a spill on the floor, trying to stay as small and unnoticeable as possible. His adrenaline rages.

The blare of the bell. Doors open. Short people with backpacks spill into the hallway. Youthful chatter, laughter. Still pretending to clean, Bridger scans boys' faces as they pass, trying to match one to the photo Sandra provided.

There.

A kid in a shirt with a dirt-biking logo walks between two other boys, talking and waving his hands as if telling a story.

Bridger stands, his face angled down, most of it under the brim of his cap. He weaves through the throng of children to the kid. "Excuse me, you're Declan Carter, right?"

The boy and his pals stop, their grins fading. "Yeah," Declan says. "Everything okay, sir?"

"I was cleaning the bathroom before and saw what you wrote in there. I'm going to give you a chance to explain yourself. If you can't, I'll be forced to report this to Principal Phineas."

"Peace, D," one of the friends says. He and the other skedaddle.

"I didn't write anything in the bathroom," Declan says.

"Well, there's a marker drawing of a middle finger in there, signed with your name," Bridger says.

"Huh? Which bathroom?"

Bridger points at one close by. "I'll show you. If you recognize the handwriting and think it was someone else, now is the time to speak up."

"I'm going to be late for math."

"You're going to have worse problems than that if you end up in the principal's office. I'll explain to Miss Lonner when we're done."

Declan sighs. "Yeah, fine."

Bridger escorts him through the hallway. It clears out as children funnel into class. Bridger opens the bathroom door.

Declan wanders in, nobody else around. He scopes the unmarked walls. "I don't see anything."

"Inside here." Bridger pushes open a stall. Declan enters. Bridger follows him in, pulling a vial from a jumpsuit pocket.

Shock streaks Declan's face. He tries to edge around the adult, but a hand clasps his throat and bashes him into the stall wall.

"Try to resist and I'll beat the shit out of you," Bridger says.

The kid stands still, shivering. Bridger opens the vial, inside a chloroform-blended liquid, dabs some onto his rag, and forces it over Declan's face. The boy's arms and legs thrash for a bit, then slow, the sedative softening his body. His eyes close.

Bridger drapes the unconscious, eighty-pound kid over his back, and inches his head out of the bathroom, confirming the hall is still empty. Crouching, he lowers himself and Declan beneath the windows on the top halves of the classroom doors, and crab-walks to the end of the corridor.

He rises, hits the exit door's metal push bar with his hip, and trots outside across the blacktop. He cuts through a strip of woods to the side street where he parked his pickup truck and loads in the abducted child.

40

Cole speaks to DEA Agent Ramirez on the phone in The Ministry of Light church. After he and Lacey heard the service end, they descended from the ceiling. He went outside, removed the wedge blocking the rear door, then locked it from the inside. He locked the front door too, plus closed the curtains on the windows to prevent anyone looking in on them.

"A statewide fugitive notice is out for you," Ramirez says. "You didn't tell me you killed a damn cop."

"The sooner you guys can get here, the sooner you can help me get the truth out."

"Jesus. All right. Looks like we'll be in town around nine thirty."

"Cool. See you then." Cole hangs up.

On the church's website, he viewed today's schedule. The next service isn't till eight PM. He and Lacey could lie low in here for a few hours.

She emerges from a doorway with a frozen bag of corn, a small kitchen behind her. "This should do the trick."

"I'm fine, really."

"You have a broken rib." She slides the cold bag under his sweatshirt.

It does feel good. He puts his hand on it. "Thanks."

"Twenty minutes on, twenty off. I'll throw it back in the freezer for you during the off time."

"Glad I'm in the company of a Doctor Mom."

"I actually used to have a crazy idea about doing that for real. Not like a medical doctor. The mind. A counselor."

"What happened?"

"Declan. A college degree, a master's, a PhD…I don't have the money or time. I could've been a doctor or a mom, not Doctor Mom."

"If you really want to do both, I think you can. You seem like that sort of person."

She blushes. He gazes into her eyes. A second passes. Then a few more. She doesn't look away. He inches his lips toward hers. She angles her head, ready for him to kiss her.

But the ring of a police siren distracts them before their lips meet. Cole pulls back a window curtain a tad. The cop car stops across the street by the deli. An officer steps into an alley, where another police car is parked. The officer peers into it.

"They coming here?" Lacey asks.

"No. But this still isn't good. Something is going on out there. I don't know what."

Earlier, his police radio picked up chatter about a 187 at the motel, which he kept from Lacey to avoid scaring her. He wonders if the activity in the deli's alley is connected.

His phone vibrates. A number he doesn't recognize, with a Texas area code, sent him a picture message.

A chain wraps seated Declan from chest to shin, a bruise on his throat, his cheeks wet from crying.

"What is it?" Lacey asks.

He doesn't answer her, checking the image for a window with

a view, a distinctive background object, anything that may hint at the boy's whereabouts. Nothing. Just Declan with a blue tarp behind him.

His phone vibrates again, a call this time, from the same Texas number. He lobs the bag of corn on a pew and paces backstage out of Lacey's earshot.

He answers. "Who is this?"

"I think you can guess."

The man in all black. Cole overheard just a few words from him before, yet still recognizes the voice.

"It's a pleasure to finally speak to you," the man in all black says.

Cole did not consider the possibility his opponents would go after Declan, not during a school day surrounded by locked doors, hundreds of students, dozens of teachers, surveillance cameras, and a security guard.

"You're really going to bring a kid into this?" Cole asks.

"What is it they say, all is fair in love and war? This game we're engaged in, you and I, I'd deem it a form of war. Would you not?"

"If you kill him, you get nothing from me."

"I know who you really are, Mister Make-Believe Inspector. I fought in the same wars as you. We are comrades. You're fully aware how things go from here. Have you heard the pop song 'Magic Marker Tattoos' by the sublime Crissy Rogue?"

Cole is quiet.

"It's about the beauty of first love," the man in all black says. "Butterflies in the stomach and kisses under bleachers and, of course, Magic Marker tattoos of each other's initials. I doubt young Declan, at only eleven, has experienced his first. It doesn't happen for real until, what, fourteen the earliest? Don't you want him to have that?"

Cole rubs his forehead. "Sure."

"If you tell me where my missing items are, Declan will not suffer. But if you choose to keep this information from me, we will take something from him, and keep taking more until you wise up. His body will be arranged in such a way that nobody could ever love him romantically."

Cole's stomach drops. He thinks about Declan's dimpled, smiling face beneath his dirt-bike helmet. Him carrying the heavy bag of sod for his mom. His matchmaker move at dinner with the Polaroid. Giving up the drugs to save him is tempting.

But Cole can't do it. If his opponents possessed the opioids, they'd spread through Timber Ridge, sure to kill kids like his teammate Igelsey's nephew. Those young deaths would be on Cole.

"I'll call you back," Cole says. He needs time to think this through.

"No you won't. Put me on speakerphone. Include the boy's mother."

"She's not with me."

A chuckle. "Yes she is. If you don't put her on in the next thirty seconds, we'll start with Declan's right thumb."

41

Lacey's face is buried in the church's curtain. She screams. She has been for over two minutes. The man in all black explained in detail what's about to happen to her son's body if Cole holds out on the pills.

She turns to Cole, her hair disheveled, her mascara smeared. Her blue eyes stare at him without breaking contact, just as they did before he went in to kiss her. But the desire in them earlier has been replaced with coldness.

He does not bother defending himself because she is right to blame him for this. If he never took those drugs, these men would never have taken Declan.

"Comrade," the man in all black says from the phone, on speaker mode on the preacher podium. "What's your decision?"

"Give him what he wants," Lacey snaps.

Cole hears another police siren. He peeks out the window into the deli's alley. The trunk of a cop car is open. The officer he saw before stares into it, shouting into his radio.

Whatever is happening across the street may turn into a problem for Cole. But he can't worry about that right now.

He returns to the podium and says into the phone, "Gator told me about you."

"What did Gator say?" the man in all black asks.

"A mindless tool, I think were the words he used to describe you."

"That wasn't very nice of him."

"He told me to watch out because you were dumb enough to do anything for him, no matter how self-destructive. Apparently he was right. Aggravated kidnapping of a minor. Pretty sure you get life for that in Montana."

"You might actually get the needle."

"Stop fucking around and tell him where the pills are," Lacey shouts, slapping the podium.

Cole glimpses her flushed face, then says into the phone, "Risking the needle to serve a man who looks down on you? I hope he's paying you a lot. How much?"

"Whatever number I say, even if astonishingly high, you're going to tell me it's low. That I'm getting the proverbial shaft. That I should release Declan and just walk away from all this out of self-respect. Correct?"

He is correct. So Cole decides to alter his approach a bit, press harder on his ego. "You should definitely walk away. But I don't think you would. I think you're scared shitless of Gator."

A snicker. "He's a businessman who grew up with a silver spoon. I doubt he's thrown a punch his entire life. That's obvious the second you meet him. Do you really know him? Or are you fibbing?"

Cole drums his fingers on the back of his neck, debating his reply. If he goes back on his original stance, he'll look like a liar. His only option is to double down on it.

"You're the one who obviously doesn't know much about him," Cole says. "Ever hear how he got his nickname?"

"Yes. His cowboy boots. Were you going to pretend it was

something spooky? Make up some anecdote about him feeding a rival to an alligator?"

Cole's fingers tap his neck even harder.

"Hold on," Lacey says. She cuts between Cole and the podium and presses the mute button on the phone. "You said in the car you never met this Gator guy."

"I didn't. This was just a tactic." He exhales through his nose. "It's not working."

"Gator cowboy boots. Businessman. Silver spoon. Never threw a punch." Her eyebrows bend. "Who does that sound like to you?"

Cole shrugs.

"Wayne Shaw," she says.

Not many people in Timber Ridge grew up with a silver spoon. Of them, Wayne Shaw is the only one who wears gator-skin cowboy boots. But he's a respected citizen. His family built the town. He wouldn't debase himself by associating with these men.

"He must be down millions with that flashy disaster Valley Gate," Lacey says. "He could be using the drug profits to prop up his business. He'd never let his family company go under."

"Are you guys friends or something?"

She looks away. "Let's just say I know him well enough to know he's very protective of his family's reputation. If he had to resort to selling drugs for it, he would."

"Huh," Cole says. "I guess it's possible."

She dabs a tear from her eye. "The good news is, I know him well enough to know he wouldn't be okay with them hurting Declan."

"I wouldn't think so either. But if what you're suggesting is true, he's obviously not the guy he seems to be."

"And Declan isn't the kid he seems to be." She takes a deep breath. "Wayne is his father."

42

Wayne enters his home from the office on the earlier side, not much to do on the job without any real estate deals in play. This is a bit of a secret relief. He never enjoyed the work, found it dry. He would've liked designing pinball machines, but was embarrassed to turn down the helm of the family company for a career in children's games. If he had the guts to deviate, his inheritance could've been invested in a successful mutual fund instead of Valley Gate.

"Hey honey," Adeline says, standing on a stepladder, stretching a mock cobweb across the archway between the kitchen and den.

His sixteen-year-old son, Jackson, sets up a plastic skeleton. "How was work, Dad?"

"Good. Real good."

Though Jackson is almost six feet tall, he still looks like a little kid to Wayne when he decorates for Halloween, his favorite holiday. A cheery smile on Jackson's face, he positions the skeleton's arms just right.

Wayne sets down his cowboy hat and walks to his family,

three cardboard boxes on the floor among them, *HWeen* scrawled on each in marker.

Wayne fishes a ghoul mask out of one and chuckles. "Remember what happened when I wore this to the Gallaghers'?"

"Duh," Jackson says. "That's why I held onto it even though it's defective. To commemorate the great plunge."

"Thanks. Because that's really something I want to be reminded of."

A few years ago, some family friends on the block hosted a Halloween party in their backyard. The eyeholes in Wayne's ghoul mask were cut too small. He wound up tripping into their garden fountain, much to the delight of the guests.

"Is the hair still a little damp, babe?" Adeline asks.

She and Jackson laugh while Wayne rolls his eyes. He grabs a big bag of fuzzy fake spiders from a box. He places some on the kitchen counter, then wanders into the den and adds a couple to the coffee table.

His phone vibrates. A message from Russell: *We have an issue.*

He situates the bag of spiders on the couch and types back: *??*

Russell: *We need to meet.*

Wayne grunts.

"You good in there?" Adeline asks.

"Yeah dear. Just a work email. One sec."

He scatters more spiders through the den while stress hardens a muscle along his spine. He pushes his fist into it and tries loosening it. No success.

"I made a batch of my fall cider," Adeline says. "Pitcher in the fridge if you want a glass."

"Looks like I unfortunately need to run back to the office." He returns to the kitchen.

"Oh."

"An old colleague of my father may have found a candidate to take over the Hadaway property. Some canned foods company from the Midwest looking to expand. The CFO is in town, fishing. He wanted to meet, get my take on the region."

"Yay, great news. Should I come with you, try to charm him a little?"

"It's okay. Stay here, finish up with the decorations. You two are on a roll."

He puts on his cowboy hat, kisses her cheek, and waves goodbye to her and his son.

43

Lacey paces the church's floor. Cole leans against a wall. When she walks toward him, he attempts to make eye contact. But she turns around and goes in the other direction.

After the call with the man in all black, she explained her affair with Wayne Shaw at eighteen. He wanted to keep his fatherhood a secret from Declan and his wife. He's deposited payments into Lacey's bank account every month for eleven years, part child support, part hush money. After she gave Cole these facts, she stopped talking to him.

He runs his fingers over the bracelet on his wrist. A lone red bead, a symbol of the red wolf, is situated among many black ones, which stand for a Native American term that can best be translated into English as "black quiet."

According to Powaw, everyone has an animal in them. But if they don't follow it, the animal will abandon them, dooming the human to black quiet, a living death.

Almost all of Cole's adult life was spent in battle, following the path of the warrior wolf. But once he got back, his path became hazy. Though he went on his mission against the bikers for his family, he also did for himself. Once again having something to fight for felt good. But now he feels more lost than ever.

"I am so sorry for what happened to Declan," Cole says. "I can imagine how mad you are at me. And I deserve it. But I agree with you about Wayne. Once they tell him what happened, he'll insist they leave Declan alone."

She shakes her head. "We don't know that for sure. Something could...get in the way." She takes a couple panicky breaths. "Give me your phone. I'm putting the cops on this."

"They're—"

"Not all of them are corrupt. Ninety-nine percent aren't. Those ones need to be looking for my son."

He lets out a long breath. She peeks out the window at the police cars across the street. Then runs toward the front door.

Cole chases her. He blocks the door just before she opens it.

In a moment, someone bangs on its other side. "Police," a deep male voice says. "Anybody in there?"

Lacey opens her mouth to say something, but Cole covers it with his hand. He flips off his police radio, which has been active about a dead cop, and drapes his sweatshirt over it.

He whispers in Lacey's ear, "The drug dealers have Declan. They have the leverage. If the cops come after them, and they're feeling cornered, they'd do anything to get away, regardless of Wayne's opinion. They could start hurting Declan until the cops backed off. I will find a better way to get Declan home safe. If I have to die in the process, so be it."

About ten seconds pass. Cole hopes the officer left.

Nope. The door starts opening. He removes his hand from Lacey's mouth.

The preacher in the green leisure suit, holding a set of keys, stands in the doorway, a lean, fortyish man in a County Sheriff uniform beside him.

Cole expects Lacey to say something to them. But she

doesn't. He also expects the cop to draw a gun. The officer just stares at him.

"This is private property," the preacher says. "You're trespassing. How did you get in here?"

"I apologize," Cole says. He nods at Lacey. "My friend and I are passing through the area on our way to Ripsaw Mountain. Being good Christians, we wanted to do our daily prayer in a place of worship. My phone said this was the closest around. The back door was open."

The preacher's head dips as if in contemplation, sweat glistening on the spots of scalp visible beneath his comb-over. He nods.

The officer walks the aisle to Cole and Lacey and asks, "Do you two mind having a look at this?" On his phone, he shows them a picture.

It's a shot from a high angle, a bit grainy. The man in all black appears to be in the lobby of Paradise Inn, the top of his face masked under his booney hat.

"Did either of you happen to see this individual in or around the church?" the cop asks.

Cole shakes his head. So does Lacey. Craving more information, Cole asks, "Is he a criminal or something?"

The cop puts his phone in his pocket. "He murdered a motel clerk. My cousin. Possibly a police officer too."

Cole pretends to appear shocked. "Lord."

The preacher says, "I saw this lost soul of a man in here just before. For some reason, he came here after leaving the motel. He may return. You are not safe here, brother and sister."

The man in all black is too smart to linger in Grinson with the police after him for murder. Cole and Lacey should be able to walk to her car without him lurking, and find somewhere else to hide.

"Thank you for warning us," Cole says. "We'll leave right away."

"One second," the cop says. He peers at Cole's face, then body. He could be trying to estimate his height and weight. "Where did you say you were from, again?"

"Didn't yet, actually. Colorado."

"How do you like Montana?"

"We're loving it."

The cop came in here looking for the man in all black, not Cole. However, the cop must've seen Cole's photo earlier in the day. Maybe because of the dyed hair, the officer didn't ID Cole upon first sight. But now that he's been around him for a couple minutes, he seems to be making the connection.

"In case I have any follow-up questions, I should take down your information," the cop says.

"Let me give you my phone number."

"Your address too. If my colleagues in Colorado need to go over anything with you in person."

"Sure."

"Why don't you just hand me your driver's license and I can copy it from there? Easier that way."

Cole taps his back pockets, pretending not to have his wallet on him.

The cop's brow furrows. He unholsters his pistol. Cole pulls the headboard post from his jeans and smacks the gun. It wings out of the officer's hand and clonks a pew.

"Come on," Cole says to Lacey. He climbs onto the stage and lifts her up by the hand.

The cop's eyes shift between them and the pistol as if he's deciding which way to go. He chooses them, sprinting ahead.

Cole shoves the podium at him, slowing him down, and slips behind the curtain with Lacey. He crosses the shadowy storage area to the back door and opens it with his hip. Daylight floods in as they rush out. He grabs the wedge he left nearby and jams it under the slab, sealing it just like the man in all black did.

The door shakes as the cop tries to open it.

A dirt hill behind the church leads to the woods. It's maybe too steep for Lacey to climb. The slope flattens two lots down, behind the liquor store.

Cole dashes into the lot with Lacey.

A young guy scrolls through his phone while barreling toward them in an SUV. The engine is quiet, a hybrid.

"Watch it," Cole shouts to Lacey while backpedaling out of its path.

She doesn't yet notice the car at her side, stopping with a confused expression.

Cole jumps back into its path, pushing her out of the way. With a gasp, she stumbles into the clear. But the SUV slams Cole's right hip.

Pain rocks through his body. He tumbles across the parking lot.

"Oh man, my bad," the driver says, exiting his car.

Cole rises and steps toward the woods. But falters on the injured hip. Climbing the hill will take longer in this condition.

"You okay?" Lacey asks.

"I'll call an ambulance," the guy says.

By now, the cop could've given up on the church's back door and raced out the front. He is sure to eyeball the surrounding properties. Cole doubts he can make it up the hill in time.

He looks around. A dumpster.

If the SUV driver witnesses him and Lacey get in, he may blab. Cole needs to scare him off.

"I don't want your help," Cole says. "Now get out of here before I punch your teeth out."

The guy scampers to his car and zips away. Cole limps to the dumpster and heaves up the lid, the stench rising. He climbs in, helps in Lacey, and closes it.

44

The tightness in Wayne's back worsened. He sits in his parked BMW at the secluded spot where Russell requested they meet, Bemknock Trail, a hiking destination the town shut down for a falling-branch hazard. Ropes block off the entrance.

A Harley interrupts the quiet. In his rearview mirror, Wayne notices Russell pulling up, the only other person in sight. Russell parks beside the BMW. Wayne steps out onto unlandscaped grass blanketed in dead leaves.

"Why couldn't we do this over the phone?" Wayne asks.

"I have to give you something."

"And it'll make this problem go away?"

"Yes."

"What the hell went wrong now?"

"Chill out. I'm here to help."

Wayne adjusts his cowboy hat. "This thing with Cole Maddox has been…a lot for me."

"I know." Russell moseys to his side and nods at the pine-tree-covered slopes in the distance. "When I'm feeling jumpy, sometimes I look out at the mountains and count to ten."

"I'm not in the mood for any…zen…thing. Can we just get to what went wrong and how to fix it?"

"You'll feel better. I promise. Try it."

Wayne laughs, then shakes his head. "Screw it. Why not? Why not at this point?" He peers at the mountains and counts in his head.

One. Two. Three. Four.

A sharp pain in his gut. He looks down. Russell jammed a knife into his belly. Blood swells on Wayne's suede jacket.

A look of sympathy is on Russell's face. "You're doing great. Stay still. It'll all be over soon."

Wayne lurches forward. His hat falls off.

"A business decision was made above you," Russell says. "That's all this is. I wish there was another way."

Russell swipes the blade to the side, razoring Wayne's internal organs. Wayne crumples to his knees, then face-first to the ground. He lies trembling, watching his blood dye the leaves around him.

His body begins numbing. The ache in his back goes away. Then everything does.

45

Lacey gags. The dumpster smells like spoiled milk. Cole is crammed beside her in the darkness on trash bags, some bulky and rigid, others mushy and wet.

After they climbed in, Cole turned back on his police radio, put on an accent, and reported a sighting of the fugitive Cole Maddox in a maroon pickup, driving east toward the highway.

The diversion worked. He heard a siren go on by the church and move eastward. Not many cops would be on patrol in a small town like Grinson. A few must be occupied with the man in all black's murders, and another is dead. But more from the county should arrive soon. Once they fail to spot Cole on the highway, they'll scour downtown for him, sure to check the woods and the liquor store's dumpster.

"It has to be you," he says to Lacey. "My photo has been in the news all day. Yours might be soon, but I didn't see anything on the internet yet. Between now and then is your chance."

She sighs. He just gave her a brief tutorial on the art of pick-pocketing. If she can lift the keys from a customer in the liquor store, Cole hopes they can flee the immediate area by the time the customer finishes shopping and reports the theft.

His phone vibrates. The light from the screen illuminates Lacey's bloodshot eyes. He opens a picture message from the man in all black.

A guy in a suede jacket lies on the dirt, blood extending from his midsection onto leaves, half of his face visible.

Wayne.

Cole reads the accompanying text: *Hello comrade. You and the waitress are to meet me at 329 Fallinstaff Street in Stoud Hollow. There you will tell me where the goods you stole are. An associate will stay with you while I check if you are fibbing. If you try anything silly, or don't arrive within 30 minutes, Declan will experience the things we discussed before.*

Cole takes a deep breath of the rancid air. He sees no alternative to driving to the address. As for giving up the buried drugs once there, he sees no solution yet.

"Things just changed," he says to Lacey. "Not for the better." He enters the meetup address in his Maps app. "We have someplace to be in thirty minutes. It's twenty away. You have ten to get in there and come out with a set of keys."

"Did they hurt Declan?"

"Not yet. But nothing is stopping them anymore."

He expects her to panic. But she does the opposite. She poises herself, her posture straightening. She appears to slip into a new headspace. She lifts the dumpster lid.

46

Lacey opens the door of White Horn Liquors, a bell chime announcing her entry. Cases of beer sit in fridges along the wall to her left, a few aisles of wine in the store's center, bottles of hard booze checkering the wall to the right. A man in overalls pays the female cashier, five other customers floating around. Based on Cole's quick pickpocketing lesson, Lacey tries to choose the best target.

Focusing is difficult. She can't stop thinking about how frightened her baby must be. So much other heavy knowledge was dumped into her head today too. You're unsafe, leave your house now. Your ex is a drug dealer. Your neighbor with the nice smile, whom you were developing feelings for, is reckless. Cole meant no harm, yet caused a lot.

She takes a deep breath. Three customers in here are male, two female. Per Cole's lesson, men are easier marks because they keep their keys in pockets versus harder-to-access purses.

Of the three guys, one wears a puffy jacket. What's in his pockets would be hard to see. According to Cole, he's a no.

Thinner coats are on the other two. A middle-aged one pushes a shopping cart with some wine while a twentysomething clutches a vodka bottle. Without a cart, and just one free hand, the younger guy could grab just one more bottle, maybe two. He should be done shopping soon. But the man with the cart could be stocking up for a party. He could be here a while.

She veers behind him, pretending to read labels on a rack labeled *Sauvignon Blanc*. A slender man with gelled hair, he wears a jacket that falls to the center of the seat of his jeans, the bottom halves of his back pockets visible. Something is in the right, but appears bigger than a set of keys. A wallet maybe.

She'll need to get around him for a glimpse of his front. Cole suggested she use her sex appeal as a distraction on a male mark. She lifts her hand to pat down her disheveled hair and make herself presentable. But when the leather sleeve rises to her face, she catches a whiff of the dumpster on it.

Sexy can be tough if she smells like this. She needs a better distraction. Anxiety pounds in her chest.

She again lifts her hand to her head, but not to fix her hair, instead to mess it up even more. She yanks strands and rubs her mascara, giving herself the look of a crazed drifter.

The man reaches for a bottle of Cabernet. She juts her hand across him and points at it. Putting on a fast, shaky voice, she says, "This stuff will do you right if you mix it with NyQuil. Ever try that, mister?"

She eyeballs the front pockets of his jeans. They look empty. But the two in his coat don't. A long rectangular protrusion to the right one. Like a phone. A shorter bump to the left. Like a key fob.

"No," the guy says, sneering. "Haven't tried that." He loads the bottle in his cart and moves down the aisle.

She walks alongside him, her hip against his. "I can't really afford any of the shit in here, but I like looking."

"That's…nice." He scopes a shelf of Malbec.

Once he grabs one, she says, "Oh, yeah, that one is real good. Mind giving me some money so I can get one too?"

She reaches across him for a bottle. While he recoils his head, she slips a hand into his coat pocket. She plucks out the set of keys and tucks them under the sleeve of her jacket.

"Enough, miss," he snaps. "Can you leave me alone? Thank you."

She gives him a dirty look and storms out of the store. She aims the key fob at the handful of cars in the lot and taps the unlock button. The lights of a tan Honda sedan flash. She kicks the dumpster twice, signaling to Cole.

His head lifts from the bin. She waves him toward the car and opens the driver's door. He nods a couple times as if proud of her, then hops out and dashes to the sedan.

47

Bridger tries to enjoy his late lunch from McDonald's but the screaming interferes. The kid, Declan, is chained up in his basement. His repeated cry for "Help" carries up to the kitchen.

Bridger's phone vibrates. A picture message from his girlfriend. She's in the break room at the tobacco shop where she works, flashing him. *Your turn* is typed beneath.

He dunks a fry in a puddle of ketchup he squirted on his burger wrapper. Chewing, he tries to ignore the kid and think about his girlfriend's tits. But can't.

"Fucking A," he mutters.

He grabs his cup of Sprite and descends the stairs to the basement. Declan struggles against his chains with a childish grunt. He locks eyes with Bridger from across a secondhand pool table.

When Bridger was tasked with the abduction, he felt sorry for Declan, but never questioned completing the job. Since then, he heard Wayne Shaw turned his back on this kid just like Bridger's dad turned his back on him. Now Bridger can't help but see a part of himself in the boy.

"Whuh…what…why am I here?" Declan asks.

Bridger removes the lid from the Sprite. "You thirsty?"

Declan nods. Bridger guides the cup to his lips and eases in the cold soda. The muscles in Declan's little throat gulp.

"You did nothing wrong," Bridger says. "Nothing to deserve any of this."

"Then why'd you do it?"

In an ideal world, someday Declan would find someone like Russell to teach him things and the kid would turn out okay. But that future won't happen.

Russell gave Bridger explicit instructions on how to finish this job. Even though Bridger is compelled to free the kid, he can't let Russell down.

"Your neighbor stole something from some people," Bridger says. "This is a way for them to get it back."

Declan is quiet a moment. "Cole?"

Bridger nods.

"Cole isn't a thief," Declan says. "There was a mistake."

"No. It's complicated."

Declan stares at the pool table, a pensive tilt to his head. "What then? You're going to keep me here until Cole gives back the thing he took?"

Bridger wishes it were that easy. "Nobody is here but me. Don't tire yourself out yelling for help. I'll check on you in a little."

"Cole wouldn't want me to stay here. He'll—"

"You're not leaving here."

"Then Cole will come for me. He's…my friend."

"He's not your friend. He's just some guy trying to screw your mom. I knew plenty of guys like him when I was a kid. He doesn't give a shit about you. He's not coming for you."

The kid snivels. A tear rolls down his cheek.

Bridger wanted to be straight with him, but now can't bear to look at him. He goes upstairs to numb himself with cocaine.

48

Cole lies in the backseat of the stolen Honda to avoid the gaze of any cops who might be on the road. Lacey drives to the man in all black's meetup address in Stoud Hollow.

"I don't want all that fentanyl sold in Timber Ridge either," she says. "But my son is more important. When we show up, no more of your...tactics. Just do what they ask so they give back Declan."

"I see where you're coming from. But unfortunately I have a feeling they won't be giving back Declan."

"What?"

"They'll demand the drugs first. If they get them, I doubt their next step will be making good on their side of the deal." He takes a deep breath. "It'll be tying up their loose ends."

"What loose ends?"

"Like the clerk in the motel."

"Witnesses?"

"Witnesses."

"So you're saying Declan...oh my God."

"And me. And you."

Her chest puffs up and down. He puts a comforting hand on her elbow. She rips it off.

He gives her a half minute to just breathe, then says, "I have a plan."

She doesn't seem to even hear him.

"Lacey," he says, "I might be able to fix this."

She doesn't reply.

"You play a minor role," he says. "Even if you can't stand me, I need you to at least hear me out. This is our only hope."

He explains his plan. She nods when he's done, but still says nothing.

The sadness he felt at Quinn's birthday party could've been his spirit trying to tell him something. Though wolves can be lone, they thrive in packs. For him to find a path in the civilian world, he may need a family of his own. Though he just met Lacey, he saw the potential for a future with her.

But it may be gone.

She drives through a canyon, fields of withering wildflowers on both sides at the base of mountains with craggy apexes piercing the gray clouds.

No other vehicles go this way. A wooden fence borders a tract of empty land, posts and rails dilapidated. The paved road turns to dirt. At its end stands the remains of a small barn, its siding warped, a hole in the roof.

Next to it is the man in all black's Toyota alongside a pickup. Lacey parks and holds her face in her hands for a moment. They step out, Cole still limping from the SUV hit.

The barn door clunks open, revealing a frizzy-haired, late-twenties man in a thermal shirt and Freedom Riders vest. He's average height, but must weigh about two fifty, a bit of a gut, but most of him muscle.

He aims a compact Uzi at Cole's face and says, "Hands up."

Cole raises them. The guy pats down the pocket of his sweatshirt, then his arms. His frisking lingers on Cole's chest. "What the hell is under there?"

Cole lifts the sweatshirt and flannel, exposing the bandage around his gunshot wound. "Just a piece of fabric. You might've heard one of your dirty cops shot me last night."

The biker scowls at him, then kneels and pats down his ankles and shins. When his hand reaches Cole's back-right pocket, he says, "Now, that ain't fabric."

He pulls out a broken beer bottle. A clumsy liquor-store clerk must've dropped it while stocking shelves. Cole found it in the dumpster while looking for potential tools for his plan.

A cocky chuckle from the biker. He puts the jagged bottle in his own pocket, then confiscates Cole's phone. The biker pats down Lacey with a lewd grin, rubbing her ass in the process. The sight irks Cole, but he maintains his composure. He cannot become sidetracked.

The biker leads them into the barn. It's dark besides the dim daylight dropping in through the hole in the roof with the rain. The heavy door closes behind them. A couple mice scuttle.

The man they hid from at the church, now wearing a red jacket, sits on a rusted, overturned wheelbarrow with his legs crossed. He picks petals off a bouquet of wilted wildflowers and lets them fall to the hay floor.

His green eyes peer into Cole's. They somehow seem both full of life and dead.

"The dipshit tried to sneak in a broken bottle," the biker says.

"Tsk, tsk," the man in the red jacket says. He paces to Lacey, plucks a flower from the bunch, and slips it behind her ear. "It was sad to see that chic silver fox Wayne go. But the powers that be in Mexico thought it was a good idea I move to Timber Ridge to take his place." He struts to Cole. "Stabbing me with a broken bottle wouldn't be very neighborly of you."

The opioid scourge in town was bad enough with Wayne lead-ing. If a shrewder boss like this took his place, it'll worsen.

"Would you like a flower too?" the man in the red jacket asks Cole. "With those flowing locks, high cheekbones, and sharp jaw, not to mention your nice physique, it would give you the air of a Nineteen Sixties surfer. A terrific look."

"I'm more of a skier."

Angel nods at the biker, who tugs Cole to a vertical post, pushes down on his shoulder, and says, "Get your ass on the floor."

Cole sits on the rotting hay. With zip ties, the biker binds his ankles, and wrists behind his back, and secures his torso to the post with rope. He does the same to Lacey at a nearby post. Then he licks her cheek. She whimpers.

Cole glares at him.

"Ohh," the man in the red jacket says to Cole. "That makes you mad, doesn't it? Your face is getting red."

"Let me just tell you where the drugs are so we can be done with this."

"You think you're better than me, don't you?"

"I never said that."

"But you're thinking it. I'm in the narcotics business, so I'm beneath you, right?"

"I have a screenshot of the GPS coordinates saved in the photos on my phone. I'll give you the PIN. All—"

"We're in the same business you and I. You don't spend as much time in Special Forces as men like us if you're not. Hunt-ing. That's our business. Whether it's me hunting for missing opioids or you hunting for revenge for your brother, makes no difference. Winning the contest is what matters. Sinking your teeth into your prey at the end and tasting blood." He points at the biker. "You want my associate Marvin's blood, don't you?"

Cole is silent.

"You're no better than me, comrade," the man in the red jacket says. "We're the same."

49

Marvin the biker spins his Uzi around his finger while pacing the barn. He's on hostage-watch duty while the man in the red jacket drives to the latitude/longitude Cole showed him.

"Excuse me," Lacey says to Marvin. "My son must be really scared right now. Can I talk to him on the phone just to tell him this is all going to be over soon?"

He kneels in front of her and strokes her thigh. "How about you, doll? Are you scared too?"

Cole's pulse picks up. When he came up with his plan, he didn't envision Lacey's distraction would cause anyone to fondle her.

"Don't be scared, baby," Marvin says to her. "Let's have some fun."

While Marvin's attention is on her, Cole shifts his torso to the side the few inches the rope allows, then drags his back across the post he's tied to.

Marvin runs his hand up Lacey's thigh to her white tee shirt and says, "Let's see what we're working with." He pinches some fabric and nudges it up. She clenches her eyelids. He lifts the shirt to her neck, exposing her C-cup breasts in a pink bra. "Good. Very good."

Cole keeps dragging his back across the post. His gunshot bandage flaps to the side from the friction. A triangular, three-inch object frees from it. It dances down his back, out of his shirt, and onto the hay.

A glass shard. He knew they'd search him before, knew they'd find the broken beer bottle. It was just a plant to convince them they disarmed him, and cause them to let their guard down some. Back in the dumpster, he snapped off a piece of glass big enough to cut through restraints, yet small enough not to have protruded beneath the bandage during a frisking.

Marvin squeezes Lacey's breast and says, "You like the way I feel?"

Cole grips the shard and cuts into the zip tie around his wrists. It splits. With his unrestricted hands, he rotates the rope around his torso, the knot now in front of him. He undoes it, the coil easing around him. He cuts the zip tie off his ankles.

"How about a kiss?" Marvin asks Lacey, creeping his face to hers. She tucks her chin to her chest. "Your bitch is being stubborn," he says. He looks over his shoulder to Cole.

Marvin's eyes widen. Cole runs toward him with the glass shard swaddled in the fabric of his sweatshirt, raised like a stake.

Marvin backpedals. He aims his Uzi. Cole kicks his arm before Marvin can pull the trigger. The Uzi flails but remains in his hand.

Cole slashes the glass at his face. Marvin dodges it. The shard collides with the post Lacey is tied to and pops out of Cole's hand. She screams.

Marvin points the gun at Cole's head.

Chracha. Bullets fly out as Cole ducks.

He springs upward, driving his shoulder into Marvin's stomach. Cole rams him into the wall. Wooden boards rattle in a cloud of dust.

Marvin aims the gun down at Cole's back. But Cole grasps his wrist and yanks him to the floor.

Marvin elbows Cole in the jaw and tries to aim again, but Cole bear-hugs him from behind, pinning Marvin's arms at his sides. Marvin tries to bust loose. He is strong, but Cole's hands stay clasped.

Cole's feet push against the floor, muscling them toward the overturned wheelbarrow. If he can bang Marvin's head into it, he can faze him enough to take the gun.

The interlocked men roll. Cole's cheek lands on the spiky hay. He heaves heavy Marvin into another roll. Then another. The wheelbarrow is just a yard behind him.

"Get off me or I mow her the fuck down," Marvin says.

At this angle, he lacks a shot on Cole, but has a clear one on Lacey.

Cole freezes. "Okay."

"Then let go of me, dickhead. Now."

Cole unhooks his hands. He leaps backward. Marvin stands and turns to him. Cole lands on the other side of the wheelbarrow.

Chracha. Bullets nail it, Cole crouching behind it for cover.

He throws it at Marvin. It knocks him off balance. Rounds blast into the wall just to Cole's side. Tottering Marvin adjusts his aim, but Cole punches him in the mouth before he's hit.

Marvin's back thumps the floor. His front tooth is now missing. Cole slams the wheelbarrow over his arm, trapping the gun while inflicting trauma to his elbow joint. Marvin winces.

More bullets fire, but the metal dome contains them. Cole reaches under it, pries the Uzi from Marvin's weakened arm, and points it down at his face. "Tell me where the boy is."

"Fuck off."

"You guys aren't getting the drugs. The DEA is seizing them by the end of the day. Don't die for this cause."

Marvin spits at him, saliva dotting his jeans. Cole stomps Marvin's other elbow joint and hauls him across the barn by the collar of his Freedom Riders vest.

Cole presses a knee into Marvin's back, grasps the glass shard off the floor, and digs it into the flesh just beneath Marvin's hairline.

The biker's injured arms slap at Cole, but lack the vitality to budge him.

"Where's the boy?" Cole asks.

"Suck my dick."

Cole drags the sharp sliver backward, peeling off an inch of Marvin's scalp. The biker howls in agony, his blood reddening the hay.

Nearby Lacey looks appalled.

"Tell me where he is," Cole says, "or I keep going."

Nothing but heavy breathing from Marvin. Cole grinds off two more inches of frizzy-haired flesh.

"Okay, you fucking maniac," Marvin yells. "Ah. Fine. Just stop. Stop."

"I'm going to tie you up. Then drive where you say. If Declan isn't there, I'm coming back to strip your whole head. I'll let you feel that pain for a while before putting a bullet in your brain. You understand?"

Marvin pants some more. "He's with one of us. Bridger Sparks."

"Address?"

"Deep River Ave. I don't know the number. It's a shitty house toward the northern end of the block. Green."

Cole zip-ties Marvin's wrists and ankles and ropes him to the post he was bound to. He smashes Marvin's phone with a boot heel and takes back his own.

With the glass shard, Cole cuts off Lacey's restraints. She stares at the blood dripping from the tip.

50

Lacey steps out of the driver's door of Marvin's pickup at Timber Ridge's Kenohoe Glen Rest Area. The Honda, sure to be reported stolen by now, is back at the barn. She turns to a building with refreshments and bathrooms, a destination aimed at tourists on their way to Yellowstone National Park.

Cole sits up in the pickup's backseat and waves to her. She does not reciprocate, peering at him with confusion in her expression as if unsure what to make of him as a human being. She wanders past an old couple in Yellowstone caps and goes inside.

Leaving her here alone is a bit of a risk. But for the protection of her body and psyche, he does not want her anywhere near the upcoming confrontation with this guy Bridger.

His sweatshirt hood up, Cole climbs into the driver's seat, pushing the thought of Lacey's coldness out of his mind. He must focus. He pulls back onto the highway. His hip, rib, and chest throb, the brawl with Marvin aggravating his injuries even more.

He exits and veers toward Deep River Avenue, a street in the section of Timber Ridge with the cheapest housing. He crosses railroad tracks. This neighborhood was never nice, but deteriorated in the years since he's been. He passes a mangy stray cat, a couple boarded-up houses, a man in ragged clothing pushing a cart of cans in the rain.

Near the northern end of the Deep River is a green house. A Harley in the driveway. Though grisly, the scalping seems to have been effective. But Cole's time for completing his plan is running out.

In about fifteen minutes, the man in the red jacket will realize he was provided a false pill-burial spot and instruct Bridger to begin dismembering Declan.

Cole doesn't park in front of the house, but five down, out of view. He limps up the street with Marvin's Uzi in the back of his jeans under his hoodie.

He cuts onto the lawn of Bridger's next-door neighbor, then weaves through trees and bushes and hops a fence onto Bridger's property. The house's paint is faded, the gutter bent, a few roof shingles missing. Cole crawls to a front window.

A McDonald's bag on a counter, a ratty couch, a poster of a girl in a bikini straddling a motorcycle. No people visible on the first floor.

He shimmies up a drainpipe. The shoddy mount almost busts from his weight. He stretches his hands to a thin ledge beneath a second-story window.

He inches up his head for a look inside. A stained rug. A couple beer cans lying on it. Nobody is in this room, yet he hears R&B music in the hallway beyond its open door. Someone could be up there.

Cole skulks to the front door. On the ride from the barn to the rest stop, he assembled makeshift pick tools from a paperclip in the Honda's glovebox and one of its windshield-wiper blades.

He removes the tools from his pocket and fiddles with the lock until breaking it. Aiming the Uzi in front of him, he gives the door a slow push.

Though music plays upstairs, the volume is low. He takes

light steps up the staircase, edges his head into the hall, and swivels it to the right. Nothing but a shadowy bathroom. To the left, a door is halfway open, the music spilling from it.

He presses his back to the wall and sidesteps to the doorway. He leans forward a touch, gaining a line of sight into what appears to be a bedroom. He sees a man's bare ass. A pair of white briefs wrapped around a pair of thighs. A back covered with tattoos.

Cole, with a partial reflection of the guy's front in a mirror, recognizes him from The Knotted Vine. Holding his phone, Bridger seems to be posing for a dick pic.

He may have a baby face, but not body. His thick, well-defined muscles are wrapped in veins, almost no fat on him. He could be on steroids.

Bridger snaps a photo and snorts white powder off the back of his hand.

Cole, with a clear shot on his head, lifts the Uzi.

Then he feels a chomp on his calf.

He glances down. A ferret is biting him. It yelps, the noise rising just above the music.

"You all right, Wilhelm?" Bridger says.

He spins around, his jaw dropping at the sight of Cole. He slams the door.

Cole can't blanket-fire through it until verifying Declan isn't in there.

"Declan," Cole screams.

A few seconds later, he hears a muffled voice from the basement. He can't make out its words, but can tell it's Declan's.

Just before Cole fires, the bedroom door rips apart from the other side. Drywall debris hits Cole's cheek, a blast echoing through the hallway. The wall just to his side is shredded from buckshot.

Bridger has a shotgun.

Cole rolls into the room with the stained rug and beer cans. He juts the Uzi out of it and squeezes the trigger.

Chracha, chracha, chracha. The bedroom door bursts apart, slivers flying about.

Cole moves the Uzi left to right, up to down, flames flashing from the muzzle as shell casings spring out its side. Rounds rip through what remains of the door.

After a couple seconds of unrelenting fire, Cole eases off the trigger and marches toward the room along the wall, the weapon still at the ready in front of him in case Bridger somehow survived.

Cole pushes open the door. Shards of glass are clumped at the base of the mirror. The cocaine-topped night table is chewed up. The waterbed is leaking. No Bridger in sight.

Cole enters the room, spinning toward the blind corner. No Bridger. Cole opens the closet. No sign of his opponent.

A chilly breeze. The window is open.

Bridger must've escaped through it after firing a cover round.

Cole eyes the driveway. The Harley is still there. He hears the garage door opening. And sees Bridger go back inside. To maintain leverage, he must want to grab Declan before fleeing.

Cole runs out of the bedroom as fast as he can with the limp. He descends the stairs to the first floor. He hurries to the basement door and opens it. Around the foyer's corner, fast footsteps approach.

The butt of Bridger's shotgun whacks the Uzi out of Cole's hand. It slides into the room with the bikini poster.

Bridger points the shotgun at Cole. But Cole yanks the barrel upward before it blasts. *Budoom*, a round tears a hole in the foyer's ceiling. Fragments of it shower on them.

Cole twists the shotgun, trying to force it out of Bridger's grasp. Bridger resists. Cole pounds Bridger's forehead with the butt.

The blow doesn't knock him out as Cole hoped. The cocaine and steroids must have him too jacked up to pass out.

"I'm gonna make a mess of you just like I did to your pussy of a brother," Bridger says. He shoves Cole through the basement doorway.

Cole's back slams onto the hardwood staircase. His pinkie finger snaps against a step. Bridger smashes onto Cole's left leg, cracking its shinbone.

The impact rattles the shotgun from their mutual clutch.

Cole somersaults backward onto the landing and bangs into the wall. The gun slides down the bottom half of the staircase and skids onto the concrete floor.

Cinderblock walls, a tarp. Declan.

"Cole," he calls out.

Cole tries to stand, but his shattered shin prevents him. He tumbles down the rest of the steps.

Bridger leaps over him toward the weapon. But Cole tugs his ankle, collapsing him to the floor.

They wrestle, colliding with the pool table. Cole punches Bridger in the face and crawls to the gun.

"Look out," Declan shouts.

Cole glances over his shoulder.

In Bridger's hand is the purple 4 ball from the pool table. He hurls it at Cole's head. Cole ducks out of the way. Bridger reaches into a pocket for another ball while Cole grabs the pool cue leaning against the table.

The yellow-and-white 9 ball flies down at Cole. He deflects it with his forearm, slowing it some, but it still hits his head with enough speed to daze him. He drops to his side, blood from his lip spattering his sweatshirt.

Bridger sprints around him toward the shotgun.

Cole swings the pool stick into Bridger's kneecap. The cue's top foot splits off. Bridger trips, but stays on his feet.

He keeps running to the shotgun. Cole lunges after him, but is unable to catch up on his shattered leg. Bridger snatches the weapon and turns to aim it.

Cole glimpses the spiky-tipped broken cue in his hand. He throws it like a javelin. It soars through the basement.

And penetrates Bridger's throat.

Bridger totters into the wall, the cue bobbing as blood gushes from his jugular. The shotgun falls from his hand. A moment later he falls to the floor.

A croak from his mouth. Then another. Then no more. His body is motionless.

Cole takes a few deep breaths.

"He told me you wouldn't come," Declan says. "But I told him…I told him you were my friend."

Battered Cole crawls to him. "Bet."

51

C ole eyes the chain around Declan. "Did that man hurt you?" Cole asks.

Declan stares at Bridger's corpse. "I'm…I'm okay."

"I don't know many people who would've gotten through that. You're a really brave dude."

Declan takes a deep breath. In a panicky voice, he asks, "Did these people come for my mom too?"

"She's safe." Cole looks around for a key to the padlock securing the chain, but doesn't see one. "We need to get out of here. A neighbor could've heard the guns go off and called the cops."

"Shouldn't we tell the cops about this?"

"No." Cole crawls to the shotgun by Bridger's corpse and crawls back to Declan with it. "Long story." Cole spins the chain, putting the padlock behind Declan. "This won't hurt. I promise."

Budoom. Buckshot and lock fragments streak through the basement.

Cole pulls off the chain. He nods at his cracked left shin, a bloodstain over his jeans from the bone's puncture of his flesh.

"It's going to be hard for me to walk. Mind doing me a favor to help?"

"Anything."

"Grab the end of the pool cue I broke off before."

Declan runs down the foot-long piece and hands it to him.

Cole tears off his sweatshirt and winds it around the cue fragment, against his calf. He ties the sleeves, forming a splint. He stands. Pain burrows up his left leg. He lifts its foot, shifting all his weight to the other leg, which is still far from stable from the SUV collision. He wobbles a bit.

Declan circles his arm around Cole's waist for support.

Cole gives him an appreciative nod, then hops on his right foot to the staircase. Gripping the handrail, he hops up the steps one by one.

He reaches the first floor. Holding the basement door for balance, he says to Declan, "There should be a black gun in the next room. Do me another favor and grab it."

Declan darts out of sight and returns with the Uzi. Cole tucks it his jeans. With Declan's arm looped around his waist, Cole hops out the front door. The rain stopped, yet the sky isn't clear, a fog sprawling across it.

Cole gazes at Marvin's pickup. It's five houses away. A lot of ground to cover on a shattered shin. With Declan's help, Cole moves about a dozen feet.

The soft noise of a police siren. It's growing, coming from the direction of the pickup. By the time Cole hopped by five properties, the cops would be sure to spot him.

"One last favor," Cole says. "Run inside and get the motorcycle keys."

"I don't know where they are."

"Check counters, tables, shelves."

"On it."

Declan breaks from Cole, who topples to the asphalt without

the support. Cole crawls to the Harley in Bridger's driveway. His palms scrape the pavement. He mounts the motorcycle.

The police siren gets louder.

"Got 'em," Declan says, sprinting out the front door with a set of jangling keys.

Cole holds out a hand. Declan underhand tosses the keys to him. Cole pats the seat behind him. Declan climbs onto the bike and clutches him.

Cole starts the engine. He zooms out of the driveway, the police siren just around the bend. He hooks a high-speed right onto an intersecting street, zipping away before being seen.

52

Angel's shovel clinks against rocky soil. Its noise is the only one around. He kicks the shovel deeper into the earth, dumps the dirt, and keeps digging.

Soon a pile of soil rests beside him, a hole in front of him. No pills peek up from the ground. They could be lower. He could dig more. But his gut, which tends to be right, tells him Cole Maddox fucked him.

At the barn, Cole did indeed direct Angel to a screenshot on his phone of GPS coordinates. But it could've been a decoy. He could've deleted the real screenshot and added one for this spot on a remote face of Sacagawea Peak, a mountain in the northern half of Gallatin County.

Angel stakes the shovel into the ground, rests an elbow on the end, and calls Marvin.

Right to voicemail. Angel calls Bridger.

Ringing, then a recording, "This is Bridger. If you wanna get me quicker, just text. Peace."

Angel gazes at the red sun descending in the sky toward the gray hills.

He dials Russell. The call connects.

"I was about to hit you up," Russell says. He sounds choked up. "I think Cole Maddox just killed Bridger."

Angel taps his thumb against the shaft of the shovel. "He did, did he?"

"That kid was like a son to me." Russell yells something inaudible. Then a crashing sound as if he pushed or kicked something over.

"What do we know for certain?" Angel asks.

After a moment, Russell returns to the phone. "Sandra just stopped at Bridger's house. It's a shit-show crime scene. He's… definitely gone. The cops didn't get Cole."

"And the boy?"

"Missing."

"And Marvin?"

"I tried him. Not picking up."

"You're closer to the barn than me. Drive there, check on him, let me know the status."

"Yeah." Russell hangs up.

Angel runs scenarios in his mind for what could've transpired, how Cole could've gone from captive of Marvin to killer of Bridger. Each scenario would require extreme skill.

Angel detects movement near a grove of trees. An animal wandering alone. The bottom of its coat is white, the top gray, its eyes yellow. It stops and stares at him. Angel stares back.

A cold wind blows, a rustle to the pine needles behind the wolf. Something about the animal brings Angel peace. In its eyes is love, the kind he'd imagine from a pet. He treads the rocky terrain and sits beside the wolf.

It does not move beyond the slight swells and contractions from its breathing. Angel places his hand on its soft coat and pets it.

Angel once loved a woman, in Afghanistan. Her name was Sabira. He'd visit her in her apartment at night, where they'd drink black-market wine. After the bottle was done, she'd play music and teach him to dance.

But after knowing her just a month, he lost her. While she walked to the market one morning, a car bomb went off, killing her and four others.

Angel uncovered the identity of who planted the bomb. And waited for him in his home that evening. When the man and his wife returned, Angel cut off the man's eyelids so he was forced to see, and decapitated his wife in front of him. Angel then skinned him alive before decapitating him too.

The wolf's eyes gaze into Angel's as if to tell him something. Angel tries to understand what. But can't.

The wolf walks off into the woods. Angel remains on the ground, thinking of Sabira.

In about thirty minutes, his phone vibrates, Russell calling him back. Angel stands and answers. "What more do we know?"

A throaty exhale from Russell. "I just found Marvin. Cole and the chick got away at the barn."

"Marvin's dead?"

"No, but he sure ain't doing well."

Cole must've somehow escaped his binds, subdued Marvin, and administered pain for Bridger's address. Angel would've done the same.

"Marvin may not be dead now," Angel says. "But he needs to be. He just betrayed us."

"We don't know that for sure."

"If I'm going to be running this business, I cannot have bendable men in my employ. I trust you'll take care of this for me."

"Our numbers are dropping. Earl still hasn't showed up. Then...Bridger. A crew our size can't afford to lose another guy. Marvin fucked up, yeah. And deserves to be punished. But not killed."

Angel does not reply. Silence for a few seconds.

"All right," Russell says. "I'll…handle it."

"Thank you."

"We've got another problem too."

"Do we?"

"Goddamn DEA. Cole told Marvin they're confiscating our stuff. Sometime today."

Angel takes a deep breath.

"Feds, man," Russell says. "Serious shit. Sandra and her guys could maybe throw them off our trail for a second. But that's about it. There's just…that's a lot of heat."

"What're you implying, Russell?"

"Look, all right. We didn't know Cole was some…Delta Force whatever. That's been plenty bad already. If we keep coming at him, with feds around too, more of our guys are going to die. Maybe we just…take a loss on this. Your boys in Mexico can send another shipment for us to sell."

"My associates in Mexico won't be too keen on sending us more product on credit until we recover the product they already sent on credit."

Russell is hushed.

"If the DEA seizes the missing stash," Angel says, "and ties it back to us, we will all end up in federal prison for a long time. We must get it before them."

Russell grunts. "It's gonna be tough at this point, not gonna lie. We lost the boy and the woman. We've got no leverage over Cole."

"Then let's get some."

53

Angel's Toyota cruises through Bozeman toward a glass-and-chrome building. He passes a sign on its well-groomed lawn, *Gallatin Health Center*.

Coming here was a last resort. At large hospitals like this, police officers are on premises twenty-four seven. And, unlike in Timber Ridge, no cops in Bozeman are on the drug dealers' payroll.

Angel parks in a three-story structure for visitors and exits the car, leaving his wallet inside on purpose and resting the key on a tire. In the hospital, he doesn't want any identifying objects on him. An arrest here would be a worse predicament if he were armed, so he leaves his 9mm and wrench umbrella behind too. He unties his ponytail and rumples his hair. Long strands settle over his face.

He walks into the building with just his burner phone in his pocket. He follows a sign for *Reception*. About twenty people move about a hallway, some with balloons, some in scrubs, others wheelchairs.

Angel puts on a weak gait, then crumples forward. For added

realism, he does not extend his hands to brace his fall, allowing his face to smack the linoleum floor.

"Oh my," a woman says.

Angel shakes on the tiles, drooling, faking a seizure. People stop and watch.

"Code blue," a guy shouts.

A stretcher is rushed over. An Asian man and Black woman in blue scrubs, *RN* badges on their waists, struggle to lift Angel's muscle-heavy body onto the stretcher. Once they do, they wheel him down the hall.

The male nurse shines a penlight in Angel's eyes, then turns him on his side and asks the female, "You see a medical ID on him?"

She bunches up the jacket and shirt fabric on Angel's right wrist, then left, as if to check for a medical bracelet. She sticks her hands in his pockets.

"Nothing," she says.

They wheel him into a room.

"Cushion the skull," the male says.

She sets a pillow beneath Angel's convulsing head. They watch him shake for another half minute.

He slows. Then stops.

The penlight returns to his eyes. "Sir?" the male asks.

Angel says nothing for a bit. Then, "Uncle Paul?"

"Excuse me?"

"Did you make sure the potatoes are crispy? You know how mad Mother gets when the potatoes are soft."

The nurses glance at each other, then step away from him.

"Do you recognize him?" the female asks in a soft voice. "Has he been admitted before?"

"Not familiar. He could be a faker looking for drugs. I'll get a doctor in here. We'll probably run an EEG to see if he's for real and go from there." He leaves.

"Uncle Paul?" Angel says.

"Uncle Paul will be back in a little bit," she says.

Angel rubs the sleeve of her scrubs top. "Looks comfy like pajamas. I want to be comfy too."

She grins. "Hang on." She exits and returns with a hospital gown and slippers. "Think you can put these on all by yourself or do you need some help?"

"Mother says big boys can do things all by themselves. I'm a big boy."

"Yes, you are. I'll give you some privacy to get changed and check on you in a few minutes."

She leaves. He removes his outfit and puts on the gown and slippers. Holding his phone, he cracks the door and peeks into the hallway. No sign of either nurse. He treads the corridor, appearing to passersby as just a frazzled patient. He finds a door to the stairs and climbs to the second floor. Then veers to room 243.

Patient Jay Maddox's.

Angel requested the room number in his initial meeting with Wayne, who happened to come here to visit for genuine reasons before Cole inserted himself into their business.

Angel reaches the door labeled *243* and knocks. "I think there was a mix-up with the rooms. If anyone is in here, you need to move. This is mine now."

He listens for a response from a medical practitioner who may be inside tending to Jay. To Angel's delight, no voice comes.

He turns the knob with a handful of gown fabric, avoiding fingerprints, and enters. The room is silent besides the soft hiss of the ventilator hooked up to comatose Jay. An IV stand is at the left of his bed, a monitor with vital stats at the right.

Angel closes the door, then curtains, shutting out the darkening sky. With his phone, he takes a picture of the still patient.

He sends it to Cole with the text: *Bravo for your performance at the barn. I suspect you already sent the real lat/long to the DEA. Open up that message on your phone and take a screenshot of it. Include a delivery timestamp so I can be sure you don't make a fake. If I do not receive what I'm requesting within 2 minutes I will scoop out an eyeball from your brother's skull.*

Angel waits bedside, staring at Jay's unresponsive face. Unconsciousness is fascinating. That mysterious grayness between life and death.

A minute passes. Then two.

Angel hooks an index and middle finger into the shape of a claw and lowers them to Jay's left eye.

Dudoing. A clank rings through the room. Pain ripples through Angel's head.

He lurches forward onto the mattress. He attempts to regain his footing, but his surroundings rock a bit.

Over his shoulder, he sees a thin old man with long hair clutching a bedpan. Behind him is the open door of the bathroom, where he must've been hiding.

A flash of recognition in Angel's dazed head. From the social media photos he found researching Cole's family. Powaw.

"Help," Powaw screams toward the hallway. "Police. Help."

An on-site Bozeman cop should be barreling in within seconds. Angel steps to the window, his only hope for a successful escape.

Powaw charges at him. Angel evades another swing of the bedpan and slaps it to the floor. Powaw throws a punch. He's stronger than he looks. Angel dodges it, clasps Powaw's wrist, and launches him through the window.

Angel moves the curtains and peers down at the courtyard. The old Indian lies on the grass with his eyes closed. A woman in a wheelchair wails while the man pushing her gawks.

Angel grabs his phone and Jay's pillow and leaps out of the window with the pillow over his shoulder, aiming for a vine-wrapped trellis. He bangs into it. The cushion absorbs some of the impact, but pain still radiates through his arm and neck.

The woman in the wheelchair screams again. Angel rolls to one of the trellis's vertical posts and climbs down to the grass. A thorn on a vine must've cut him, blood trickling from his chest onto his hospital gown.

He bolts out of the courtyard and turns the corner of the building.

A voice behind him asks, "Sir, everything all right?"

Angel stops. He turns to a freckle-faced policeman about twenty-five. The cop must not yet know who Angel is. This guy may not be a problem, rather an opportunity.

"No, Officer," Angel says. "Some crazy man just threw me out of a window. I'm trying to get away before he comes after me. Please...do something, help me."

"Just...uh...one second, sir."

The young policeman takes his radio off his belt and relays a sighting of an assault victim.

A voice replies, "The thing in two forty-three. I'm in there now with Wilkes. Another guy didn't walk away from it."

Angel scopes the vicinity. Western larch trees by a redbrick retaining wall. Some people tread a walkway a few dozen feet away, none paying attention to him and the cop at the side of the building.

While the officer listens to his colleague on the radio, Angel sneaks behind him and unclips his gun holster.

The cop lets go of his radio. It bounces on the ground away from him. He clasps Angel's wrist before he pulls the pistol out of the holster.

The officer looks toward the walkway as if to shout to a pedestrian, but Angel slaps his hand over his mouth. The cop pulls his nightstick off his belt. He hammers it backward into the front of Angel's kneecap.

Angel's leg gives out, his knee sinking to the grass. His hand slips from the cop's mouth, but his other remains on the holstered gun.

"Help," the cop yells toward the walkway. He turns and swings the nightstick at Angel's head.

Angel ducks, then yanks the cop to the ground. Angel's arm is squashed between the falling man and the grass, its fingers loosening from the pistol.

The cop unholsters the gun while Angel pries the nightstick from him. The cop turns onto his side, aiming. Before he can fire, Angel nails his forehead with the stick.

A gob of saliva shoots out of the cop's mouth. Angel hits him again, hard enough to knock him out, but not kill him.

While Angel reaches over the cop to take the gun, he hears a woman's voice. "Everything okay?" she calls out from the walkway, too far away to see them.

Angel drags the unconscious cop behind the retaining wall. He strips off the man's blue police uniform, long-sleeve Under Armour shirt, shoes, and socks, then removes the hospital gown. Angel changes into the Bozeman PD uniform. It's tight, but passable. He holsters the gun and puts the gown on the cop.

"Anyone back here?" the woman asks, her voice close.

Angel emerges from behind the wall with a friendly grin. "Hi ma'am."

The lady turns to him. She wears a sweatshirt with a horse on it. "Did you hear someone calling for help, Officer?"

"A patient from the psychiatric wing seems to have had an episode." Angel loops the out-cold cop's arm around his neck and lugs him around the wall.

"Gosh," she says, grimacing.

"Thank you so much for your concern. But I have it from here."

She waves. Once she walks off, Angel carries the cop toward visitor parking.

54

Cole sits on a rock among the trees surrounding the Kenohoe Glen Rest Area, his body pulsing with pain. A head aching from a pool ball, a shot chest, a broken rib and finger, a demolished shinbone.

After learning his opponents were brazen enough to infiltrate Timber Ridge Middle School, he felt they may do the same at the Gallatin Health Center. So he texted Powaw, asking him to come out of hiding to watch Jay. Upon receiving the scooped-out-eyeball message from the man in the red jacket, Cole called Powaw to intervene. He hasn't heard back despite five attempts.

He tries to focus on positives. Lacey and Declan are off the grid. After Cole escorted the boy here on the motorcycle, a friend of hers from a nearby town picked up her and Declan. They'll spend the night at the friend's.

Lacey did thank Cole for saving her son. But she still seemed tentative in Cole's presence, still unsure what to think of him. Figuring she needed some space from him, he didn't ask to join her at her friend's house. He'll hide in these woods.

His phone vibrates. His hand rushes to it. Powaw isn't calling. Melanie is. He answers. "What's up?"

"What the hell have you gotten us into?"

He's quiet for a moment. "Did anything—"

"Jay's doctor just called me."

"Is Jay all right?"

"The call wasn't about Jay. It was about Powaw. The doctor just…saw him."

"Did the doctor see Jay too? Are you sure nothing happened to him?"

"Something sure did happen. Someone threw Pop out a fucking window."

A knot in Cole's gut. "Is he…is he?"

"Somehow he survived. He's in surgery now."

Cole lets out his held breath.

"But he might not make it," she says. "I know you're trying to put away the men who assaulted Jay. But this vendetta of yours has gone too far. End it now before they find my little girl and throw her out a window next."

"I understand how hard this must be on you, Mel. But it'll all be over soon."

"Not soon. Now. Please Cole. No more. Quinn is crying in the other room. I have to go." She hangs up.

He sets his elbows on his knees, dips his face in his hands, and closes his eyes. Despite Melanie's argument, he still can't bring himself to give up the drugs. The daylight gives way to night, about seven PM, two and a half more hours till the DEA arrives. Cole needs to wait things out for just a little longer till the feds end this calamity.

The woods are quiet besides the drone of cars on the highway. Then a police siren cuts above the thrum.

He gazes between leaves at the stone-walled rest stop a few dozen feet away, the flags of America and Montana flapping on poles near a two-pump fueling area. Its lights spinning against the foggy dusk, a Timber Ridge police cruiser pulls into the parking lot among cars, RVs, and semitrucks.

This must be a coincidence. They must be here for a reason besides him, maybe some shoplifter.

But when the two cops emerge, they gravitate to Bridger's parked Harley.

The police radio on Cole's waist has been turned off to not draw attention to him in the woods. Truck drivers frequent rest stops, many with CB radios. One could've heard about a homicide victim's missing motorcycle and called in a sighting of a matching plate number.

An officer enters the building while the other paces the property outside. He shines his flashlight into the brush about fifty feet from Cole, who debates sneaking away from here through the woods. But no. He wouldn't get far on his decimated shin before they found him.

His only chance at a getaway is the Harley.

He hops into the parking lot on his good leg. He falls, gets up, and keeps going.

A man leaning against a Saab, smoking a cigarette, stares at him. "You need a little help there, pal?"

The voice catches the cop's attention. His flashlight beam shoots onto Cole.

"Stop," the officer yells. "Cole Maddox, Kenohoe Glen rest area," he says into his radio.

Cole mounts the motorcycle.

The cop runs at him, aiming his pistol. "I said stop, asshole."

Cole digs Bridger's keys out of his pocket and turns on the engine.

"Shit," the cop says. He dashes to his cruiser, heaves open the door, and dives behind the wheel.

Cole zips around a row of parked cars toward the split in the trees where the lot merges with the highway on-ramp.

He closes in on it. So does the squad car. Just before Cole escapes, the cruiser lunges in front of him, blocking the path.

Cole brakes. The trees on the rest stop's perimeter are too tight together to drive between. But behind the building is an open field. Cole may be able to reach it through a rear exit.

He spins a hundred eighty degrees on the bike, rubber screeching on pavement, and drives to the building.

He eases off the gas as a motion sensor parts the glass double doors. He rolls inside on the growling machine, about a dozen people around, a couple gasping.

A high-ceilinged space with a food counter, a coffee counter, a mini-mart. A side exit, no rear-facing one though.

But Cole does see a rear-facing window, a big glass semicircle on the second level.

"Shut that Goddamn engine off," a male voice hollers.

Cole glances over his shoulder at the second cop sprinting at him. Cole twists the bike's throttle grip, accelerating toward the staircase.

A bathroom door opens. A man steps out. Cole winds around him, bashing into a stand of tourism pamphlets. They flap like erratic birds.

Cole rides up the steps. A woman on them backs against the railing, dropping her food tray.

His body bumps as he rises. He jolts onto the second level. A family of four sitting at a table gawks at him.

Cole takes a deep breath tinged with the taste of exhaust. He cruises to the end of the tile floor as the cop races up the steps.

Burumm, Cole's engine hums as he charges at the window. An expression of shock on the policeman.

Cole angles his head down. His front wheel smashes the glass. The outdoor air touches his face. The motorcycle glides, slivers of broken window floating among it.

Cole kicks his legs backward. He rises a few inches off the

seat. His front tire nails the ground, then a split second later, his rear one. He bangs back down on the seat. Pain quakes along his spine.

A shoulder of his flannel is shredded, a dab of blood on the skin beneath. In a sideview mirror, his makeshift leg splint lies unraveled in the field.

He turns the throttle grip and booms toward the road. He merges onto the four-lane highway and notches the bike up to seventy-five MPH.

A minivan in front of him lumbers along. He veers around it and accelerates to ninety. He cuts off a Mercedes. The driver flips him off.

Cole's dyed hair blows, wind crackling in his ears as he blazes at a hundred MPH. In his mirror are the lights of the police car.

To elude a checkpoint up the highway, he should get on side streets. A tractor-trailer in the left lane and Ford Explorer in the right hem him in, forcing him to decelerate to about sixty. A concrete divider borders the blacktop on one side, the forest the other.

The cops are gaining on him.

Cole makes out a small gap between the front of the tractor-trailer and rear of the Explorer. He weaves through it, avoiding a crash by inches. The truck's horn blares.

Back at a hundred MPH, he whooshes to the next exit. He slows at the ramp, but not much. The road curves. He leans into the turn, the Harley slanting left, his knee just above the pavement. He brings the bike into a drift, its tires skidding yet under control, then hurtles onto a residential street.

In his mirror, the police car barrels onto the exit ramp.

Small houses on large swaths of land buzz by Cole. He nears a traffic signal at an intersection.

The light turns red. Through trees and fog, he looks for

another vehicle's headlights on the cross street. He sees none. He rides to the red light, ready to bolt through it.

As he nears the intersection, he gains a better view. Though no other motor vehicles approach, a guy on a bicycle does.

Cole slams his brakes. He dodges a collision, yet the Harley wobbles.

No chance to rebalance. He jumps off. The tipped motorcycle slides across the asphalt, sparks spraying from the exhaust pipe. Cole plummets onto the grass and tumbles. The Harley's front fork whacks a tree.

New aches eat into his body. Elbow, wrist, knee.

"Holy fuck," the bicyclist says, scurrying to him. "You okay?"

Cole peers past him, the blue-and-red police lights nearing. Cole crawls to the Harley. The loose Uzi is too far to grab. Though the bike took a beating, it still seems functional, its engine humming.

Standing on one leg, he hoists the motorcycle upright, then climbs atop it. He drives back onto the pavement. The front wheel's bent fork sends him on a screwy trajectory.

He dips the Harley back into a wheelie. Relying on just the viable rear tire, he moves in a straight path, though not as fast as he's been.

He cranes his neck, peeking around the bike for a look ahead. He's not far from Steelhead River, where he fishes with Powaw and Jay. Its current can whisk him deep into the wild, away from the cops.

With the wail of the police car at his tail, he makes a right toward the river. The bike bowls over an orange plastic barrier. It whirls along the pavement. A sign detaches from it.

Road Closed.

The blacktop curls around a bend. Cole sees the bridge over the river is under construction, chunks of it missing, a crane and stacks of supplies by it.

No way to cross it.

He loosens up on the throttle and lowers the front tire to the pavement. It jerks to the side. He yanks the handlebars the other way, but can't steady the bike. He brakes. The swerving worsens.

The Harley staggers toward the bridge. The surface is nothing but a gaping grid of beams, beneath them a deadly drop to the boulder-strewn river.

He jumps off the motorcycle. His arms flail. They clamp around a bridge beam. His chin whumps the metal. His legs dangle.

The Harley sails through the air with a slight spin. It plunges onto a big rock. Its fender blows off.

"Get off there," a voice yells.

Both cops stand beside their parked cruiser, aiming their pistols at him.

On the other end of the bridge is a grassy hill leading to the water. It's steep, but he should be able to slide down it without getting hurt. He grapples along the horizontal beam.

"The bridge on Trussard," a cop says into his radio. "Go to the eastern edge. Over."

With his injuries, Cole doesn't move as fast as he'd like. Water crashes beneath him. A crow circles above him.

He's almost there. He sucks in a big breath and keeps moving. Left hand, right.

The ring of a police siren swells through the woods in the direction he's going. He climbs a little faster, his risk of falling a little higher. He reaches the spot where this end of the bridge meets land.

The cruiser stops short, a pebble zinging into the side of Cole's neck. He swings his good leg onto the earth and rises. On a single foot, he teeters between the ground in front of him and the lethal fall behind.

Forward, back, forward, back, forward. He collapses onto the dirt. While he crawls toward the grassy hill, a burn consumes his back.

Over his shoulder is a cop with a stun gun. A projectile is stuck in Cole. It's attached to a wire, voltage zapping through it.

He spasms, losing power over his muscles. The policeman fastens cuffs around Cole's wrists.

55

The young Bozeman police officer Angel abducted quivers in the passenger seat of the Toyota. His forehead is lumped from those nightstick whacks back at the hospital.

Angel still wears the guy's uniform, *J. Thibbs* on the nametag. They're in a quiet alley, nothing around the parked car but brick facade. The sky is black.

Officer Thibbs's phone, on speaker mode, rings on the dashboard. The DEA Supervising Special Agent from Billings answers and says in a gruff voice, "Marlowe. Who am I talking to?"

"Hi sir," Angel says, pointing the cop's gun at him. "This is Jonas Thibbs with the Bozeman PD. I got your number from Rebecca Clayhorn at the DCI Narcotics Bureau."

"What do you need, Officer?"

"I've been investigating some gang activity in Gallatin County. My confidential informant mentioned you guys were stopping by Timber Ridge tonight."

"Is this about those bikers?"

"The Freedom Riders, sir."

"I was briefed on that this morning. Big score from what I saw on tape. We're happy to throw our hat into the ring."

"We just had an assault in one of our hospitals that seems related. I'd like to connect with the agents you're sending to town, hopefully be of some help. Do you happen to know who's coming?"

"Ramirez, one of my best, he's running point on this."

"Do you have a cellphone number for Agent Ramirez?"

"Give me a second." In a moment, he returns to the line and provides a number.

Angel memorizes it. "Thank you. If you wouldn't mind, could you please let him know to expect a call from me?"

"Thibbs, Bozeman. Got it."

"So long, sir."

The DEA supervisor hangs up. Angel opens the phone's settings and disables the PIN requirement.

Thibbs's trembling intensifies. "You can keep the phone if you want, it's fine."

Angel smiles.

"Should I just get out here or do you want to drop me off somewhere else?" Thibbs asks.

Angel stares at him.

"You...you said all you wanted me to do was get that guy's cell number from Rebecca, and you'd let me go."

Angel keeps staring at him.

Fear invades Thibbs's expression. He opens the passenger door and tries to escape. Angel grabs the hospital gown, forces him back into the car, and clutches his testicles.

"You...you are...you're a...fucking sociopath," Thibbs mutters.

"No." Angel is quiet for a moment. "Sociopaths don't feel anything around other people. I do." He breaks Thibbs's neck.

Angel still remembers the rush he felt as a child killing his neighbor's cat. He did it a few months after his grandfather burnt him with ash in Mexico. At eighteen, Angel joined the army for the unique opportunity to kill a greater animal, the human, without legal consequences. Over the years, he's gotten so good at eluding the law, he now ends human lives for much higher pay for the cartel.

He glances in the rearview mirror, confirms nobody else is in the alley, then loads the corpse into the trunk.

Back in the vehicle, he taps the email icon on Thibbs's phone. He opens the inbox for his Bozeman.net email address and scans through recent messages, stopping on one from a sender with *Patrol Captain – Police Command Staff* as the title in his signature.

Angel sends an email to this man: *Hi sir. Not feeling too good. Been vomiting. Going to take the rest of the day off.*

-Jonas

He starts the engine and pulls out of the alley.

He calls Agent Ramirez.

56

Cole sits on a slab of concrete in a holding cell at the Timber Ridge police station. A hiss comes from a metal contraption that's half toilet, half sink.

No other prisoners in lockup, he's alone besides the cop who zapped him with the stun gun. Munching on a drumstick from Zeek's, the man leans against the hallway's cinderblock wall.

"Bridger Sparks kidnapped Declan Carter, an eleven-year-old boy," Cole says. "I went into his house to rescue a kid."

"Where does this kid happen to be now?"

"He's in hiding."

"So he can't come down here and make a statement? Funny how that works." The cop chomps his chicken. "My friend Officer Rick Yarvey, rest in peace, did he kidnap a little boy too before you blew his head to pieces in the Hadaway lot?" He tosses the remains of the drumstick into the cell. "Enjoy one last morsel of good food. You're gonna be forcing down prison slop the rest of your life."

He wipes his hands together and opens a door, on the other side the ringing of phones and chatter of voices in the station. He disappears. The door bangs shut.

Cole folds his arms. Yes, the DEA will soon confiscate the drugs and kick off their probe into his enemies. But he lost a lot for that.

If the probe doesn't go as planned, he could spend the rest of his life in prison. Powaw may not survive surgery. And Lacey, a potential source of harmony for Cole in the civilian world, isn't even speaking to him.

Maybe this mission of his was a mistake.

57

The door of the Timber Ridge Police Department's holding area opens. Officer Hannelson, the bespectacled ultimate Frisbee enthusiast, emerges. The last cop in here had hatred in his expression, while Hannelson looks at Cole with something closer to disappointment.

"I'm not back here as a favor to you," Hannelson says. "But the man who adopted you, some news, uh, came in that he'd probably want you to know."

Cole sits forward.

"We got word from the hospital in Bozeman," Hannelson says. "He's still pretty banged up, but made it out of surgery. He'll likely need to walk with a cane for a while, maybe the rest of his life. But doesn't face anything fatal."

Cole closes his eyes and lets out a long exhale. The knot that's been in his gut loosens, but just a bit. "Thank you for telling me. Can I talk to him?"

"It wasn't right keeping that news from you. But that's all you're getting from me." Hannelson steps to the door.

"I get one call, right?"

"You should save that for an attorney."

"I'd rather use it on my pop."

"I'm not even sure if he's in shape to talk yet." Hannelson scratches his chin. "I suppose I can ask though if you really want to skip the lawyer." He takes another step to the door.

Unlike the other Timber Ridge officers, who refused to listen to Cole's story, Hannelson may. Cole can sure use an ally in the department right now.

"I know this is going to be hard to believe," Cole says, "but Wayne Shaw has been dealing opioids in Timber Ridge."

Hannelson's feet stop. He turns around. "Yeah, and I've been drafted by the Dallas Mavericks to play center."

"Wayne was murdered today. Him, the man who threw my pop out the window, the Freedom Riders. They were all working together until the others decided Wayne was in the way."

"Eh. What're you trying to do? Create some mumbo-jumbo spectacle that'll somehow paint you as the victim in all this? It's not my job to hear it. It's the judge's. I strongly advise you use that call on a lawyer, a good one."

"I have a photo. Of Wayne's dead body. It's on my phone. I'll give you the PIN. Look for yourself."

"I doubt it. Again, not my job either way."

"I've got even more proof. Nolan Antiques. Did you see the surveillance footage the day of my brother's beating?"

"We reviewed it, yes."

"Let me guess. Sandra Evans reviewed it first."

Hannelson is silent for a moment. "What's your point?"

"She doctored whatever version is on file. She's on the drug dealers' payroll."

"Of course she is. Her cat thermos in one hand, a briefcase of oxy in the other."

"Officer Yarvey was on the take too. I only shot him after he shot me. Stop by the Nolans' house. Ask them to show you the original surveillance recording. Make up your own mind."

The hardness in Hannelson's face cracks a bit. He still doesn't appear to believe Cole, but maybe considers the possibility.

"If you're surrounded by crooked cops," Cole says, "that definitely affects your job. All I'm asking you to do is spend a few minutes checking out what I'm saying. If I'm lying, you've only lost a little bit of time. But if I'm right...you have a whole lot more to lose than time. And you need to start doing something about it tonight."

Hannelson is still for a bit. He runs a hand through his hair.

58

Angel sips coffee in Thibbs's police uniform at a window table at Timber Ridge's Gold Sparrow Diner. A new ten-gallon cowboy hat rests on his head. He buzzed off his long hair in Bozeman, plus stopped at a tanning salon for its darkest spray tan. His skin is now a deep brown.

A pair of headlights shines through the fog. A Chevy Tahoe turns into the parking lot. Two men in their late thirties in black jackets exit, a handsome Latino and bald White guy.

They enter the diner, their eyes finding the one customer in a police uniform. Angel smiles and waves. These feds from Billings would have no idea what the real Thibbs, a cop from a different county, looked like.

Angel shakes the Latino fed's hand and says, "Jonas Thibbs. Pleasure."

"Ramirez."

The second fed shakes Angel's hand and says, "O'Rourke."

The three men sit.

"Coffee?" Angel asks. "It's excellent, bold with a smooth finish, notes of honey and maple."

The feds decline.

Ramirez checks his watch. "So what's so pressing?"

"I have a possible trophy for the DEA. He's in town because of this hullabaloo with Cole Maddox and the bikers."

Ramirez steeples his hands. "I've been trying to reach Cole Maddox the last half hour. He's not picking up his phone."

"I just heard he was arrested for the murder of that cop."

Ramirez sighs, then says to his partner, "If Cole's account is accurate, it was self-defense. He can be in danger in the custody of the Timber Ridge police. We should stop by the station, see what we can do."

"By all means," Angel says. "But you might not want to go there just yet. This trophy won't be in town much longer. An out-of-state hitter from the cartel. My informant doesn't have a name, but did see him. I know the DEA keeps photos of cartel players. Maybe you can match him and arrest him before he leaves."

Ramirez taps the fingers of his steepled hands. He looks at his partner, then back at Angel and asks, "When is he going?"

"Apparently in just a couple hours. My informant is on standby, ready to talk to you. He has a good track record with tips. But if you feel he's giving you a line, I'll tell him to scram, and you can head over to the station."

Ramirez is quiet for a moment. "I'll give your guy five minutes."

Angel nods. "He can't be seen with us at a public place. I'll have him meet us somewhere close." He pretends to type a text message. "You two get to this part of the county often?"

"Dance competitions every now and then for my daughters," Ramirez says.

"My in-laws live near here," O'Rourke says. "Me and the wife spend Memorial Day weekend at their house every year. In general I get bit a lot in the summer, bugs. But for some reason, never there."

"Isn't that a hoot?" Angel says. He checks his phone, fakes

reading a text. "Okay. The lookout point on Fuster." He places a five-dollar bill on the table. "You guys mind driving? My back-seat is loaded with evidence boxes."

Ramirez nods. Angel follows them outside, putting on gloves. They all climb in the unmarked Tahoe, Angel in a seat behind the feds.

"Right on Main," Angel says. "Take it about two miles, then go left on Arrowhead Boulevard."

Ramirez makes the turns. Pine trees line both sides of the road.

"Stay on this for about three miles," Angel says, "then a right on Fuster."

The fog thickens as the Tahoe ascends the mountain. O'Rourke hums a song.

Ramirez turns right. Trees remain on one side of the street, a view of a river on the other.

"There," Angel says, pointing at a fenced overhang of the mountain.

Ramirez idles there. No other vehicles are around.

"I'll see what his ETA is," Angel says. He reaches down as if to grab his phone. But instead grabs the pistol he swiped from Thibbs.

He lifts it to the back of O'Rourke's head and pulls the trigger. Gumball-sized chunks of brain spray the passenger window.

Ramirez's jaw lowers, a mist of his partner's blood on his cheeks.

Ramirez fumbles for his holstered pistol. Angel leans forward, jutting between the two front seats, and blasts a hole through the fed's hand.

Screaming, Ramirez tries for his gun with his other hand. Angel shoots it. The tops of his middle and ring fingers blow off into the door panel.

Angel slips the pistol from squirming Ramirez's holster and chucks it over his shoulder. He does the same with O'Rourke's.

Ramirez elbows Angel in the forehead. Angel bites off his ear. Ramirez screams louder. Angel spits the frayed hunk of flesh on the center console.

"Please, just listen," Angel says. He nods where Ramirez's ear was. "Well, as best you can."

Ramirez lets out a maniacal laugh.

Angel grabs the fed's cellphone from a cupholder. It lacks a thumbprint option for unlocking, a PIN necessary.

"Enter your code," Angel says.

Ramirez still laughs, gaping at his ear on the center console. He looks out the window, darkness in all directions. "I'm not doing shit. You're going to kill me either way."

Angel pulls Ramirez's wedding band off the stub that remains of its finger. "Correct," Angel says, putting the ring in his pocket. "But after I kill you, I may or may not pay a visit to your wife and those dancing daughters you mentioned at the diner. If I do happen to visit, I'll tell you what's going to happen. I'm going to tie all three of them up in the same room. And take turns sticking myself inside them." Angel digs his gun barrel into the canal of Ramirez's severed ear. "Just like this."

Ramirez recoils. His breath picks up.

Angel pulls the fed's wallet from the cupholder and nudges out the driver's license. "Nine fifty-two Wallace Court in Billings. Just how young are—"

"Zero, eight, zero, three. My PIN."

Angel types the code. It works. He taps the email icon and scrolls through the inbox. He stops when seeing a thread with *Cole Maddox*. He finds a lat/long screenshot Cole sent.

He shoots Ramirez in the head, more brain splattering the windows.

With his own phone, Angel snaps a photo of the fed's screen. He calls Russell.

"Yeah?" Russell says.

"I need one of your guys to pick me up near the lookout on Fuster. I'll be hiding in the woods a mile north."

"Everything all right?"

"Splendid."

Angel hangs up, steps outside, and dips one of his bloody gloves into the gas tank. He slathers fuel on the feds' corpses and the dashboard. He removes a lighter from his pocket and sparks the interior of the Tahoe.

With flames thrashing behind him, he jogs north.

59

C ole eyes the clock on the jail wall. Ramirez should be in town by now. He'll hear Cole is in here. He'll do his best to get him out.

The hallway door opens. Hannelson enters. His face is pale.

He walks to the cell. "I went through your phone. And visited the Nolans."

"You believe me now?"

Hannelson hangs his head for a moment. "If Wayne Shaw and Sergeant Evans really partnered with a gang and a cartel to sell millions of dollars of opioids, that investigation is well above my pay grade."

Cole hears genuine dismay in his voice. He doubts Hannelson is a crooked cop putting on an act.

"It's not above the DEA's pay grade," Cole says. "Sync up with Special Agent Steven Ramirez. His number's in my phone. Don't tell anyone else in your department you're working with him. It's still unclear who's on which side."

Hannelson is silent for a while, as if still processing everything. "I also came back here to tell you the hospital called."

Cole's fists tighten.

"Powaw is lucid," Hannelson says.

Cole's fists loosen.

Hannelson paces to a landline on the wall, taps a few buttons, and says, "Hey Nancy. Can you reconnect me to that receptionist, have her put on that patient? Thanks." He stretches the cord handset to the cell.

Cole staggers to it.

"You need medical attention?" Hannelson asks.

Cole clutches a bar for support and takes the phone. "The cops who arrested me refused. Said I just had a couple scratches."

Hannelson sighs. "I'll give you some privacy." He leaves.

Cole, balancing on one foot, waits on hold for about three minutes.

"Hello son," Powaw says.

Cole lets the relief of hearing his voice sink in. "Hey Pop."

"I was told you're calling from jail. Is this true?"

"I owe you an apology. You were right. I tried to do the cops' job for them. And I ended up behind bars."

"No. I was wrong. For trying to stop you."

Cole is unsure what he means.

"The man who came to the hospital to hurt your brother," Powaw says. "I had the opportunity to look into his eyes. What I saw chilled my flesh. A man like that is no match for the local police."

"The DEA will hopefully take him down with the bikers."

"When I looked into his eyes, I saw his spirit. It was the same as yours. The wolf."

Cole is quiet for a few seconds.

"But I sensed he lost control of the animal," Powaw says. "In him, I saw none of the good of the wolf. Only its capacity for destruction." He lets out a heavy breath. "I hope the DEA sends the right agent to stop him."

"So do I. I'll let you get some rest now."

"Stay strong in there."

"So long."

"Bye Cole."

Cole suspends the phone over a horizontal cell bar and hops back to his seat.

Soon, the police-station chatter on the other side of the hallway door becomes louder and quicker. Cole can't make out many words from back here but can still sense a hectic mood.

In about fifteen minutes Hannelson returns. His face is even paler than before.

"What's going on out there?" Cole asks.

Hannelson presents a photo on his cellphone of a Chevy Tahoe engulfed in flames, two bloody bodies inside.

"A passing motorist on Fuster spotted it," Hannelson says. "Snapped that picture after calling nine-one-one. We were able to get the number on the plate before it melted." Hannelson takes a deep breath. "The vehicle is registered to the DEA."

Cole's been wondering why a corrupt cop hasn't tried torturing him for the pills' location. His enemies tried getting it another way.

"My chief has been on with the DEA supervisor in Billings," Hannelson says. "Backup is coming."

Cole lurches to the bars, his face inches from Hannelson's. "Billings is three hours away. We don't have till then."

Hannelson tilts his head in confusion.

"The drugs I buried," Cole says. "The dealers could know where they are now. And get to them soon. You need to move them."

"But you told me to keep all of this from the other cops in Timber Ridge."

"Yes."

Hannelson fidgets with his eyeglasses. "I want to help. I really do. But if I went into the woods alone, up against men who just took out two DEA agents, I'm afraid…I just don't see myself walking away from that alive."

He has a point. Cole can't blame him.

"Then I'll go," Cole says.

Hannelson pats the cell bars. "Forgetting something?"

"You'll need to get me out of here."

"Sure, let me fetch the key."

Cole rolls up the left leg of his jeans, revealing his nasty shin break. "Medical attention. It's my right as an inmate. Even if your chief hates me like everyone else in here, he won't want a potential lawsuit. Tell him you're escorting me to the hospital."

"What good can you do against these nuts cuffed to a hospital bed?"

"Take me to Banshee Point. Give me half an hour to move the drugs. After time runs out, whether I'm successful or not, bring me to the hospital. With your department racked on a DEA double homicide, nobody will account for us making a brief detour."

"You're asking an officer of the law to sneak an accused cop killer out of jail. If someone finds out, I not only lose my badge, but end up in that cell with you."

Cole is quiet a moment. "Last night you said you were in the Y's ultimate Frisbee league for years. Guessing you're from Timber Ridge?"

Hannelson nods.

"The man taking over for Wayne Shaw is much better at this stuff," Cole says. "He will more efficiently distribute the drugs once he digs them up. More Timber Ridge kids will OD. The higher-ups in the cartel will send a bigger stash next. It'll keep going like this. ODs will go up. Our streets will get dirtier. And no reputable company will move into the Hadaway building. Timber Ridge's economy will get even worse. Adventure Park, Gold Sparrow, Zeek's, all the places we grew up with will start closing. Timber Ridge will die."

60

Angel rides in the passenger seat of a pickup heading toward Banshee Point.

He changed out of the Bozeman PD uniform into hunting camouflage. The truck's owner, a Freedom Rider around forty, drives in a heavy-metal-band skullcap. A second biker sits in the backseat, early thirties, hair spiked into a mohawk. A cigarette dangles from his lip, smoke billowing through the cabin.

"A dawn of prosperity awaits us, gentlemen," Angel says. "We will expand first across Timber Ridge, then the county, then state. Your membership will skyrocket. The Freedom Riders will become the biggest distributors in Montana."

"I like you better than Wayne already," the older biker says.

"That shit you pulled on the DEA agents, that was ice cold," the younger biker says. "I'll roll heavy for that. You Mexicans got the ruthless moves."

No response from Angel.

"That's not, like, offensive, right, if we call you a Mexican?" the older biker asks.

"Is it offensive to call a person from Germany, German?"

"Uh. Nah."

"Well, then it shouldn't be offensive to call a person from Mexico, Mexican. The issue, however, in this particular case is that I am not from Mexico. I am from America. Same as you."

They ascend deeper into the fog among misty silhouettes of hulking pine trees. Then turn onto a dirt road, the truck rocking along. They pull into a clearing and park.

Angel turns to the younger biker and asks, "Got a smoke?"

The guy fishes a cigarette from a crinkled pack. Angel puts it in his mouth and the biker lights it.

The three men step out into the near-freezing weather. Both Freedom Riders are big, yet not quite Angel's size. The truck doors close, metallic pops resounding through the otherwise hushed forest.

Angel grasps his shovel from the pickup bed, hitches it over his shoulder, and pulls up a GPS app on his phone. He plugs in the coordinates of the buried pills.

"What we're looking for is about two hundred feet up through the brush," he says. He turns to the older biker. "We should have some time before more DEA agents arrive. If word somehow gets to the Timber Ridge PD that we're here, and some do-gooder cop shows up, shoot to kill."

"Loud and clear."

With his head, Angel motions the other guy to follow him up the hill. They walk about a hundred feet, the biker's flashlight guiding them. A shadowy lake emerges to their right, a cliff to their left.

"Patrol this area," Angel says.

"You got it, boss."

Angel hikes another hundred feet or so up the slope, aided by the light from his phone.

It dings when he reaches the GPS coordinates. He takes a long drag of his cigarette and jams the tip into his wrist.

61

Hannelson's squad car approaches Banshee Point. Cole, handcuffed in back, had to agree to certain terms for the ride.

One, Hannelson will wait down by the car, not help Cole dig up the mountain. Two, if another cop shows up, Hannelson will allege Cole assaulted him and ran off. Three, since ballistics can trace discharged bullets back to their guns, Hannelson won't loan Cole his service weapon.

"You sure about going through with this?" Hannelson asks.

Cole peers out the window, silent.

"The Banshee Point terrain is some of the gnarliest in Timber Ridge," Hannelson says. "You can barely stand on that bum leg. And these guys mean business. This just doesn't sit right. I feel like I'm driving you to the gallows."

Through the fog, a parked pickup materializes.

"Stop here," Cole says.

With a sigh, Hannelson pulls over. He unfastens Cole's cuffs and gives him a pointed-head hand shovel from the trunk. Cole, leaning against the car for support, slips the shovel in his jeans. The cold gnaws at him.

"Good luck," Hannelson says, sticking out his hand.

Cole shakes it. He hops into the dark woods and crawls among the trees, searching for one that's just right, not too thick, not too thin. One looks suitable.

With a grunt, he snaps off a branch. He knees it into two pieces, one about a foot, the other four. He removes his boots and socks. With the shorter rod, he forms a new splint for his broken leg, tying it to his calf with his socks.

The boots go back on. Clutching the four-foot rod like a hiking stick, he gazes up at the mountain. Nothing but moonlight illuminates a haze-encased pyramid of hundred-foot-tall pine trees.

He climbs toward the buried drugs. Though the two rods ease the burden on his shin, it still aches with each step.

Just before he reaches the clearing with the pickup, he kneels behind a thorny bush. And observes the darkness.

A flashlight beam to his left. The silhouette of a man roams. When the guy gets closer, Cole recognizes him, a Freedom Rider. The light glints against something in his hand. A gun.

Cole feels around for a good rock. He finds one the size of a ping-pong ball. Once the biker's back is to him, Cole flings the rock at his head. The guy stumbles forward, but stays on his feet. Cole hops to him, propelling himself with the big stick.

The biker turns around. He aims the gun at Cole. Who smashes it with the stick before a bullet is fired. The weapon leaves the biker's hand and slides down the hill.

Cole falls to his knees. He swings the stick at the biker's ankles, but the guy jumps over it. The biker distances from Cole and picks up a rock. Cole scrambles to the pickup. The rock zings just above his head and bashes into the truck.

Cole takes cover on the other side. He lays his stick on the ground, the end protruding from under the driver's door.

The biker's footsteps approach. Cole wriggles on the dirt

beneath the vehicle. From under the back bumper, he peeks at the biker. In the guy's hand is a rock the size of a grapefruit. He circles the truck. And stops by the protruding stick, shining his flashlight down on it.

As the biker crouches for a better look, Cole slips out from under the bumper. He scrambles at the guy.

The biker notices. He cocks his arm back to chuck the big rock. Before he can, Cole stabs him in the gut with the sharp-tipped hand shovel. The biker sinks to his knees.

Cole mounts him and stabs his chest. The biker tremors. Cole forces the shovel in deeper, blood spurting onto his knuckles.

The biker's breaths, rising from him as steam, dwindle. Then end.

Cole collects his stick and hikes farther up the mountain.

A second flashlight beam cuts through the mist.

62

C ole lies on the ground and peeks up the hill at another man.

"Yo," the guy says toward the clearing. "I heard noise and shit. You good?"

Cole makes out his face in the light, another Freedom Rider.

The biker descends the hill to the glow of the dead guy's dropped flashlight. He paces around the truck. And stops by the driver's door.

"Oh fuck," he says.

His beam sweeps the area. Cole advances up the mountain in a quiet crawl, watching the light over his shoulder. Just before it exposes him, he rolls behind a massive pine.

Ahead he notices a shorter tree. He waits for the light to pass, then crawls to it.

He sets down his stick at its base, climbs about ten feet up, and grasps the lowest branch.

His feet hook around it. He twists himself to the top, pine needles enveloping him. Sweat clings to his frigid skin.

Pretending to be attacked by an animal, he yells, "Get off me, get off."

The flashlight streaks in his direction. Boots pound the earth. The biker emerges, the silhouette of his mohawk against the glow.

He searches the ground with the light, his pistol in front of him.

When he crosses under Cole's tree, Cole jumps off with the shovel tip pointed down.

The biker turns away from the tree. The shovel blade misses his head, but slices his arm.

Cole smacks onto the ground. The biker's cut arm drops the flashlight. Its beam whirls onto the cliff to their side.

Pain in Cole's right hand. His index and middle fingers broke upon landing.

"What the fuck?" the biker mumbles. He sees Cole on the ground and aims the gun.

Cole stabs the shovel into the biker's foot. The guy screams and misses the shot.

Cole tackles him. They tumble down the sloped terrain toward the cliff. Cole lets go of the shovel, his hands flailing for anything solid. His right meets a tree. But his broken fingers can't latch on.

The ground steepens. Gaining speed, he closes in on the edge. About two feet from it, he grasps a big, thorny bush. He keeps himself on land from the chest up while the rest of him dangles off the cliff.

The biker slides toward him, his dropped gun a couple feet ahead of him. The pistol soars off the cliff. The biker, unable to grab anything for support, flies off too.

Just as Cole considers the biker a goner, the guy's hands clench Cole's left knee. Cole hangs onto the bush for his life as the biker hangs onto Cole for his.

Cruhh, some of the bush's roots tear out of the ground, over four hundred pounds suspended from it. Cole winces as thorns dig into his palms.

He hears a distant thud. He assumes it's the sound of the gun hitting the earth. The noise took a while to come. The drop must be at least three hundred feet.

Cruhh, more of the bush comes out of the ground. Cole stomps his right boot heel on the guy's hands. A couple fingers loosen. He stomps again. The biker's hands peel off.

But in a split second, they return. Lower. They clamp Cole's wounded shin. Cole screams. The pain is worse than that of the thorns in his palms.

He stomps some more. Again, the hands leave him and return lower. They're clasping his boot now.

Cole tries to stomp them, but they're too low for him to hit with force. The biker hangs on.

Cruhhhh.

Cole wriggles his sockless, sweat-damp foot out of his boot.

He shakes his foot. He shakes it harder.

The boot comes off, crisp air against his toes. The extra weight on him goes away. The biker lets out a scream.

It distances. Then Cole hears a faraway splat. He climbs onto solid ground and lies panting for a while, the taste of dirt in his open mouth.

He crawls up the hill and finds the flashlight, then his hiking stick and shovel.

The terrain is rough against his bare foot. He gazes up at Banshee Point's foggy peak. He may have bested those two bikers, but a worse threat should be up there. The digger. Who must be the former Special Forces operative turned drug boss, the type who'd trust nobody but himself to dig up the pills.

Cole hikes higher up the mountain.

63

Aching Cole labors to the mountain's peak. He does not want the flashlight beam to give away his location, so turned it off for now, navigating via the moon's faint light.

He stops just down from the drugs' burial spot, kneeling at the base of a tree, abandoning the hiking stick to free up a hand. His fingers feel for a good-sized rock. His palm, ripped up from the bush thorns, throbs against it.

He flips on the flashlight, a cone of light cutting between aspen trees. Nothing human in view.

In less than a second he turns off the light, then crawls through the darkness to another tree. He shines the light in a different direction. It exposes the still water of Jackrabbit Canyon Lake in the distance, but nothing human. He turns it off, moves to another tree, and turns it back on.

The pills.

More than half the bags already lie on the ground.

Pulsooh. A bang thunders through the forest.

A burst of pain in Cole's abdomen. He tips over. And pats his stomach. Wetness. Blood. He was shot.

He crawls to the back side of the tree.

Pulsooh. A round strikes the bark.

He shines the flashlight toward the gunfire. About a dozen feet away is a hint of camouflage on the edge of a big pine.

Blood from Cole's stomach drips onto dry leaves.

"I can hear you bleeding, comrade," a familiar voice says. His red jacket has been replaced with camo. "I got you, didn't I?"

"You did get me," Cole says, grimacing from the bullet searing his stomach. "Good shot. But you should've aimed for the head."

"The cute thing you were doing with the light going off and on didn't allow me good enough visibility for a headshot."

"Sorry about that."

"Look on the bright side, though. If you die from blood loss from your torso, you can still have an open-casket funeral. You'd make a beautiful corpse. I'm imagining your head on a pillow in the coffin, your locks against the white satin, a look of pure peace on that well-defined face of yours. Do you have a good suit?"

"I have one suit. I don't know if it's considered good or not."

"The right suit is a must for such an occasion. You'd look stunning in Dior, stylish yet still masculine. When I sell what I just dug up, I should be coming into some money. I'll buy you a suit as a gift and have it mailed to the funeral parlor."

The man in camo's silhouette whisks across the flashlight beam. Cole throws the rock at him, but his opponent evades it, slithering into the darkness at Cole's side.

Cole lobs the flashlight to the left.

A bullet zips toward it.

Cole goes right. He lies on the ground, masked in shadows. He slips off his second boot to minimize noise and crawls toward the sound of the last gunshot.

He sees a shape by a boulder. The man in camo crouching. He's being cautious. For all he knows, Cole has a gun too.

Cole sneaks up behind him. He dives at him and stabs the hand shovel into his back.

But it bounces off. He must be wearing a Kevlar vest under his camo.

He spins and points his pistol at Cole's head.

Pulsooh. Cole blocks the shot with the shovel blade, a loud rattle in the forest, then stabs the shovel at his opponent's face.

The man in camo ducks. Before he can shoot again, Cole bear-hugs him, pinning his arms at his sides. Cole lets go of the shovel and clasps his hands together.

The man in camo struggles to break free. He decides to roll down the hill. Tangled together, the former Special Forces operatives tumble down rugged terrain toward the lake.

Cole's back smashes onto a log. His knee bangs into a tree. His hands unclasp.

His opponent, rolling beside him, tries to aim the gun at him. But Cole slaps it out of his hand.

The men keep rolling down the steep hill and end up in the high grass on the rim of the lake. The man in camo, on top, decks Cole's face and turns around toward the hill. He tries running to it, but Cole grasps his pantleg.

Cole tries standing, but the man in camo back-kicks him in the sternum. Cole drops to the ground, his hand coming off the pantleg. The man in camo knees Cole in the chin. His head whiplashes. He falls into the cold lake.

The man in camo sprints through the grass to the hill, where his gun is. He vanishes in the darkness.

Cole can't catch up to him on his broken shin.

He taxes his mind for a solution. He hears something deep inside him. A page from *Wisdom of the Clear Moon.*

What we may search for far and wide can often be found by our side.

Earl Laughlin. He's submerged around here with his weapons.

A day of waterlogging could've disrupted the pistol, but not the knife.

Cole eyes the shadowy grass and recalls the spot where he pushed the dead body into the water. He swims to it.

He sucks in air and dives into a deeper part of the lake. He swims lower. His hand meets a solid object. He can't see it, but gauges it by feel.

The rolled rug.

His hand slides across it until meeting a bungee cord. He tears it off and digs his arm into the carpet. He feels for the Hefty bag, rips it open, and feels for the knife.

The blade slices his thumb. He lowers his hand to the handle and swims toward the surface.

He pokes out his head. The flashlight beam shines across the lake. In a moment, it moves to him, the glare in his eyes.

He hears a gunshot, then hears a bullet hit the water near him. He dives back under, cold water rushing into his mouth.

Sneaking up on his opponent is no longer an option. Cole will have to throw the knife at him. If he misses, his only two options will be dying by gunshot or drowning.

He swims underwater closer to his target. Cole's head rises out again. The flashlight beam is already on him. Cole goes back under. A gunshot. A bullet tears through the lake just above him.

The man in camo must've been following ripples on the surface caused by Cole's swimming. Cole stills himself, drifting through the chilly water. With the knife, he pushes water to his right, trying to give the impression he's swimming that way.

He looks up. Through the dark haze, a shimmer of light moves right. With gentle movements of his bare feet, Cole swims upward.

He rises from the lake and hurls the knife.

It pierces the face of the man in camo.

He crumples backward into the tall grass. He is motionless.

Cole gasps, catching his breath.

Then he notices his opponent's legs rustle.

Cole swims to the edge of the lake and scrambles to him.

The man in camo sits up. The glow of the dropped flashlight illuminates the knife jutting from his bloody face, his cheek mangled.

His eyes meet Cole's. The man in camo aims his gun.

Cole dives forward and grabs his wrist. The pistol fires, missing high. The man in camo's back hits the ground, Cole landing on him.

Cole clamps his opponent's wrist down on the grass, preventing him from re-aiming. With his other hand, Cole clutches his opponent's throat.

Blood cascades from the knife wound onto Cole's strangling hand. The vigor in his opponent's body fades.

The man in camo is dying. He seems to understand and accept this. His expression changes. His hardened battlefield glare is gone.

He mumbles something. Cole doesn't know what it means. "Sabira."

Cole keeps squeezing. Soon no noise comes from his opponent at all. The pulse beating against Cole's fingers stops.

Cole's shivering body collapses beside the still one.

64

Blood swells through Cole's flannel over his stomach. He tears off the shirt. This bullet wound's bleeding is heavier than last night's.

He wriggles his compression bandage down his torso to the new injury, restricting the loss of blood. But he's spilt a lot already. He's on the verge of passing out. He sticks his hand in his pocket for his phone. His hazy mind forgot it's still at the police station.

He crawls through the grass to the hill. Gripping trees for support, he climbs. He takes a deep breath and climbs some more. He falters, but reaches the slope's halfway point.

The tips of his fingers go numb. Without medical attention soon, he will die.

He grabs another tree and attempts pulling himself higher. But his wet hand slips. He stumbles down the hill, over roots and rocks, back onto the tall grass.

He pants. His feet have lost their feeling. Soon his legs do too. He doesn't want to die tonight. But if he does, at least he did for a good reason. He kept Declan and Lacey safe. He rid the world of the man in camo.

Though he doubts he can get up the hill, he tries again. Pain slashes into the parts of his body that haven't yet gone numb. After just a few feet, he falls into mud.

He wheezes. He prepares to die.

Then a flashlight shines from the hill.

Against its glow is a short, male silhouette.

Hannelson.

"Here," Cole calls out. But his voice is faint. Hannelson doesn't hear it.

Cole says, "Hannel—" His voice gives out.

Hannelson's light sweeps the ground, distancing from Cole.

Cole uses the remaining energy in his arms to push nearby grass stalks. They brush into the ones next to them, and those ones next to them. He creates a subtle wave that moves into the area lit by the man in camo's flashlight lying on the ground.

Hannelson's beam moves toward it. Then onto Cole.

Hannelson descends the hill. He trips, but stands back up. When he reaches the grass, he sprints. He kneels beside Cole and says, "I heard gunshots and…went back on my decision not to help." He notices the blood on Cole's torso and says into his radio, "I need an ambulance. Northwest side of Banshee Point by Jackrabbit Canyon Lake. No vehicle access. We'll need paramedics to bring in a basket stretcher."

Cole points up the hill. He sucks in a big breath of air. "Before…more…cops come. Pills. Up…there. Hide them…your trunk."

Hannelson nods and dashes up the hill. Cole passes out.

The ring of an ambulance siren awakens him.

Two guys in EMT outfits with a red basket stretcher emerge on the hill. A cop with a flashlight is behind them.

The beam finds Cole. The paramedics navigate the slope to him. They situate him on the stretcher and lift.

Their feet slip on the ascent. They pause for a break, carry him higher, stop again, then rise to flat terrain.

The waiting cop slaps a handcuff around Cole's wrist. He secures the other cuff to a metal bar on the stretcher's rim.

"Be careful with this one," he says to the EMTs. "He's a cop killer."

The paramedics peer down at Cole's face for a moment. Then carry him through the dark woods.

The policeman says into his radio, "Hannelson, where the hell are you?"

No reply.

The officer says, "Sergeant Evans, come in. Sergeant Evans."

The EMTs load Cole into an ambulance at the clearing. The cop climbs in with them. The doors close.

Sandra's voice says through the cop's speaker, "Yeah."

"I'm at Banshee Point. Looks like Cole Maddox maybe tried to escape from Hannelson on the way to the hospital. I spotted a vic lying next to a pickup truck. I believe the gentleman is affiliated with the Freedom Riders."

"Huh."

"You might want to send a team here to…check things out."

"Understood."

The ambulance drives away. Cole hopes Hannelson can stow the narcotics before any corrupt colleagues arrive.

65

Russell sits on a stool in The Knotted Vine with a somber expression. He's at the bar beside the oldest member of the Freedom Riders, fifty-eight-year-old Dugan. No other patrons are in here but a drunk at a table.

Double glasses of bourbon are in front of the two bikers. Russell holds up his and says, "To Baker and Larsen."

Dugan clinks his glass. "Goddamn legends."

They throw the booze down their throats in honor of the two bikers killed last night during the confrontation with Cole Maddox at Banshee Point. Russell points at the bartender and flashes a couple fingers.

"Baker and Larsen," Dugan says. "Then Bridger and Earl. Fucking travesty."

"Not to mention Marvin. We need to get our numbers back up."

"We still got a good group of boys. Even if not a lot of 'em. We got each other's backs. The older I get, the more I realize that's what matters. Getting someone's back and being lucky enough to have someone get yours."

The bar's door bursts open. Daylight floods in, framing a broad man in a bulletproof vest. Across the chest is *DEA*.

Aiming an assault rifle at Russell, he charges inside. Two other men in the same vest, with the same weapon, funnel in after him.

Russell hurries off his stool toward the doorway into the kitchen.

In the mirror behind the bar, he spots Dugan squaring up to one of the DEA agents. The fed clenches his arm and flips him onto a table.

Russell shoves open the double doors into the kitchen, nobody back here but a guy in a cook outfit scrubbing a pot. He gawks at Russell sprinting to the rear exit.

Russell shoulders open the back door and dashes into the alley.

His boots slam the pavement as he turns a corner toward his Harley out front. Then a rifle butt slams his forehead.

His back smacks the ground. A fourth fed stands over him, snickering in dark sunglasses.

Russell attempts to stand, but an agent tosses him back down and digs his knee into his back.

Russell's arms are yanked behind him, a zip tie tightened around his wrists. The agents lead him to the street, his head throbbing.

Two black SUVs with tinted windows are parked in front of The Knotted Vine. An agent opens a back door of the lead one and pushes Russell into a seat.

Sitting next to him is a young guy in a Timber Ridge police uniform with a bowl cut and glasses, *P. Hannelson* on his nametag. A DEA agent sits in the driver's seat, another the passenger's. They pull away from the bar.

"What the hell is this about?" Russell asks.

The fed in the passenger's seat turns to him, taps his phone a few times, then holds it up. Playing on it is a video taken behind Harris Meats, the stash of pills in the back of a van, two unconscious men in Freedom Riders vests nearby.

"What am I looking at?" Russell says. "Two guys who happen to wear a similar vest as me? What else, a couple crates of... breath mints?"

Hannelson opens a blue folder on his lap, removes a photograph of the same stock of pills in the trunk of a cop car. "All this made its way from that van to me. I handed it over to the DEA last night. Now, I'm not a scientist, but I'm pretty sure the US government has a couple on its payroll. Right?"

"Correct, Officer," the fed says. "They have these nifty tests they can do. Almost instantly, they can find out if something is a breath mint or...oh, I dunno...something you can't get at a grocery store."

"If those happen to be drugs," Russell says, "I'm glad you got them. I sure don't want that stuff on our streets."

"We know you own the butcher shop. And the van the drugs were in."

Russell is silent for a moment. "Huh. Even though that shop is here in Montana, someone once told me it's registered to some company out of Panama. I guess that means all its assets as well, vans included. A shell corporation I believe it's called. I heard it's difficult, impossible even, to get the names of any owners of a legal entity like that."

"You're right," the fed says. "Harris Meats is controlled by a company out of Panama called TR Foods. Like you mentioned, the official paperwork doesn't say much. So I decided to take a more human approach. I had breakfast this morning with the lovely old widow Mrs. Harris."

A spurt of air from Russell's nostrils.

"She never heard of a complex legal entity called TR Foods," the fed says. "But she does remember negotiating the sale of the property. With a human being. A local businessman." He points at Russell.

"We'll see what a jury says."

"If I were you, I wouldn't want to go to court."

The fed nods at Hannelson, who slips another photo from his folder. It's of Wayne's dead body, dug up in the woods where Russell buried it.

"The dogs sniffed him out by Bemknock Trail this morning," the fed says.

"What's this of, a bad hiking accident?" Russell asks. He tries to sound defiant, but his voice comes out soft.

"We used an administrative subpoena to get Wayne's cell-phone records. The mobile-tower pings from his phone put him in that area just after his wife saw him last." The fed nods at Hannelson, who slides a third photo from the folder, a shot of Russell on his motorcycle. "A residential doorbell camera caught you driving to the same area right after Wayne's BMW. Nobody else passed by yesterday but a couple locals who live on that block. Both with solid alibis."

In less than a day they have Russell by the throat. Angel killing those two feds must've caused the DEA to dedicate full firepower to this investigation.

"You're going to prison for drug trafficking," the fed says. "And so is any Freedom Rider still breathing. But if you agree to a deal with us, we can downgrade the murder charge. You can avoid the death penalty, maybe get back out while your dick still has some juice left."

"Does saying shit like that give you a little thrill?"

"I know you don't like law enforcement. So for your deal, I was thinking you rat on some cops."

Russell clears his throat. He tips his head back, curious to hear more.

"We can comb through cellphone data to get an idea of who in the Timber Ridge PD was dirty," the fed says. "But if you go on record as an eyewitness to their corruption, the case against them gets a lot stronger. Do that, plus drop any debt obligation Jay Maddox still owes you, and we'll put in writing a generous deal for you."

Russell gazes out the window at the mountains. He counts to ten.

66

Lacey tops off a customer's cup of coffee in the Gold Sparrow. "Have we decided?" she asks the table of three white-haired women.

"Pancakes, dear," one says. "All around."

"Sure thing." Lacey scribbles the order on a pad, grins at them, and veers to the kitchen.

Her new phone, in the front pocket of her uniform, vibrates. A text from Declan: *Put on channel 8.*

This last week, since Declan's return from being kidnapped, he and she have butted heads a bit. He said she seemed mean toward Cole when he dropped him off at the rest stop. Declan told her all Cole went through at that man Bridger's house to rescue him and felt Cole deserved a warmer reception from her.

Lacey tried to explain to Declan that her intention was not meanness, that adult emotions are complex, that an eleven-year-old may not understand them. Declan said that Cole is a good guy and if she couldn't see that, she's the one with the understanding problem.

She and her son made statements to the cops corroborating Cole's story while he was in police custody at the hospital.

Yesterday, through her bedroom window, she saw a car drop Cole off at his cabin. The feds must've shut down any criminal charges. Though she is happy for him, she couldn't bring herself to stop by and say hello. She's still too confused about him.

She grabs the remote control on the counter and flips the TV to channel eight. A press conference is on, in the screen's top-left corner *LIVE*, along the bottom *$2 MIL+ DRUG BUST IN TIMBER RIDGE*. A table displays many clear bags of pills.

The four male customers at the counter glance at the TV. "Turn on the volume if you don't mind?" one asks Lacey. She does.

On the screen, men and women with news-station microphones huddle around a podium with the DEA seal.

Soon, a trim, fiftyish man in a dark suit steps to the podium and says, "Good morning. I'm Nicholas Marlowe, DEA Supervising Special Agent out of Billings, Montana. Today I come to you with news both celebratory and sad." He hand-signals at the narcotics. "The DEA recently oversaw one of the largest opioid seizures in Montana's history. This should be a forceful first step in controlling the drug problem in Timber Ridge and its surrounding towns."

A male patron in the diner applauds. A female on the other side of the room whistles. Soon, almost everyone in the place claps or cheers.

"Trafficking arrests have been made for various individuals associated with organized crime," the DEA official says, "in addition to officers of the law who conspired to support these individuals."

He hand-signals to his left. The camera pans to an easel holding a poster with a pair of smiling faces on it, a Latin man and White one. "On a tragic note, two of our own were lost in this effort. We honor the memory of Special Agents Steven Ramirez and Mason O'Rourke." The official dips his head for a moment of silence.

He then says, "The DEA also owes its appreciation to a civilian who was instrumental in this seizure. He wished to go unnamed. But I'd be remiss not to mention the profound role he played. I'll now take any questions."

The reporters' hands shoot up. The diner patrons react to the press conference. Lacey overhears talk about acquaintances whose kids overdosed, hopes for a new corporation to buy the Hadaway property, and the possible identity of the mysterious civilian who helped the DEA.

She stares at all those confiscated drugs on the TV. Cole told her about the stash, but so much that day was just a blur. Seeing the deadly pills in front of her creates a visceral effect. If not for Cole, they would be inside the bodies of Timber Ridge citizens.

Yes, Cole can be a violent man. Yet she cannot picture another kind of man defeating those drug dealers. Maybe taking them on wasn't a reckless, kneejerk response to his brother's attack. Cole's choices could've come from a sense of duty. Not just to his family but the whole town.

She asks the cook, "Mind making me a scrambled egg burrito to go, ahead of the other tickets?"

"You got it, Lace." He grabs an egg and cracks it on the griddle.

She finds a waitress she's friends with and asks her to cover her section for a little. Soon the cook rings a bell.

With the bagged burrito, Lacey drives her Volkswagen toward her house. But instead of continuing to her driveway, she pulls into Cole's.

A hammer in his hand, he stands with his back to her in his garage beside his in-progress canoe. A big plastic medical boot is strapped over his jeans. Three of his fingers are in splints, gauze over his palms. Underneath his denim jacket, she assumes, is a collection of stitches and bandages for all his other wounds.

He looks over his shoulder to the noise of the approaching car. His eyes spark once they meet hers through the windshield. But the rest of his expression remains in limbo, as if he's unsure about the reason for her visit.

She steps out of the car with the bag. "I brought you some breakfast."

His eyes hold on hers for a couple seconds. Then his face eases into that nice white smile of his. "Thanks." He takes the bag. "I actually have something for you too." He walks into his house, a bit off-balance on his medical boot.

He returns and hands her a business card. It's for an attorney.

"Who's this?" she asks.

"I hired a defense lawyer last week to help unwind all the legal trouble I was in. After I was released, I asked him if he could recommend any colleagues who specialize in family law. He gave me the card for that woman."

Cole was aware Wayne had been paying her in secret every month. Now that Wayne's gone, those payments will stop. A lawyer could help.

"I appreciate the recommendation," she says, "but I'm going to have to save up for a while before I can afford the retainer for someone like this."

"No need. I already took care of it."

Her head goes back in surprise. She eyes the card again and runs her thumb over the raised lettering. She slips it in her peacoat pocket. "Thank you."

"I was maybe going to tell you later today after your shift." He looks away. "But I wasn't sure if you were ready to, you know, talk to me again."

She wraps her arms around his neck and kisses him.

He kisses back.

In a few seconds, their heads part.

"I heard them talking about you on TV before," she says.

"The DEA actually offered me a job. In Billings."

"Oh. You…took it?"

"Nah. I'm done fighting. I'm good here in Timber Ridge."

With a smile, she turns to the Volkswagen. "See you after work maybe?"

He nods. She waves at him over her shoulder.

67

Cole sets a tray of burgers he just barbecued on his kitchen counter. His doorbell rings. He paces into his foyer in his bulky medical boot. He's been in it for almost two weeks. Though his shin still hurts, he can tell it's healing. His other injuries are too.

He opens the door. Powaw stands on the stoop with a cane.

"Am I the first one here?" Powaw asks.

"No. But they've got a much shorter trip."

Cole points at the den. Lacey and Declan are on the couch.

"This must be Lacey and Declan," Powaw says. He shakes their hands. "I've heard plenty about you."

"You too," Lacey says.

Cole is happy the lawyer he recommended seems to be working out. She already met with Adeline Shaw's attorney. Instead of operating Wayne's troubled real estate business, Adeline plans to liquidate all its holdings. Pending the result of a paternity test for Declan, Lacey is owed the continuance of child support for seven years.

In addition, Declan is entitled to a portion of his late father's wealth. Once the assets are sold, the two attorneys will negotiate a lump sum payment. It should be quite sizable. With Declan's financial future established, Lacey won't need to keep putting aside money from her diner paychecks for his college tuition. Cole urged her to use that money on her own tuition and enroll in online classes. She did.

"He's here," Melanie says in an excited voice.

She enters the house with Quinn in a stroller. Behind them is Jay.

Everyone applauds as Jay steps inside.

"Take it easy," he says. "All I'm doing is being awake. You're all awake too. I'm not clapping for you."

They laugh. Jay introduces himself to Declan and says hi to Lacey, mentioning how he recognizes her from the diner. A two-inch scar runs down his forehead from the padlock on the end of the chain Bridger Sparks whacked him with. But the internal damage has healed.

The GoFundMe donations from Timber Ridge residents covered a solid chunk of his hospital bill. Powaw handled the rest, refusing to let Cole put in a dollar. Jay's loan from the Freedom Riders, keepable without interest per Russell's plea deal, will go to Melanie's eye surgery.

Jay grabs a burger. He takes a bite and says to Cole, "It's good. But your party-grilling skills still aren't in my league."

"Neither are my party-costume skills. I was expecting spandex."

"I had a nice little number picked out. But you were hosting and all. And I decided not to show you up with all that sexiness."

Cole chuckles. "Fair enough."

Melanie pops a bottle of champagne. She pours glasses, one for each adult, and hands the first to her husband.

Jay kisses her. She passes the second glass to Cole and the third to Lacey.

Jay says to Cole, "So I saw that canoe you got going in the garage."

"It's getting there."

"Must be taking a while with you all bandaged up. I'll give you a hand. It'll go quicker."

"Appreciate it."

Jay hugs him. Powaw filled Jay in on all that happened while he was unconscious, all that Cole went through to put away the men who hurt him. Jay does not have to say the word thanks. Cole feels it in the hug. Jay squeezes for a few seconds before letting go.

"We're building a boat together, Pop," Jay says as Powaw walks by.

"The canoe, yes." Powaw nods at Lacey and Declan across the room and says to Cole, "You'll enjoy the water better if you go out with company."

Cole sips his champagne and smiles.

THANK YOU FOR READING BLACK QUIET!

W e hope you enjoyed it as much as we enjoyed bringing it to you. We just wanted to take a moment to encourage you to review the book. Follow this link: **Black Quiet** to be directed to the book's Amazon product page to leave your review.

Every review helps further the author's reach and, ultimately, helps them continue writing fantastic books for us all to enjoy.

You can also join our non-spam mailing list by visiting www.subscribepage.com/AethonReadersGroup and never miss out on future releases. You'll also receive three full books completely Free as our thanks to you.

Facebook | Instagram | Twitter | Website

Looking for more great Thrillers?

Stopping a tragedy makes him a hero... ...But was any of it real? After surviving a public shooting and saving someone in the process, Alex Baines's life is forever altered... Video of the tragic event spills across social media. Major newspapers are interested. Even movie deals are being offered. This could be a career boost for the neuroscientist and meditation guru. But Alex's marriage hangs on by a thread. His leg is shattered from a bullet wound. Evidence is piling up that the attack was not random. And while police hunt down the gunman, Alex's wife Corrine begins to worry someone is after her and her two children, too. All the while, state Investigator Raquel Roth has never seen a case like this. A criminal who makes major mistakes, yet seems to have a master plan. And is someone pulling his strings? As Roth and her partner race to figure out the madman's motive, signs point to an even more sinister plan in the works. If only they can untangle the mystery and stop the disaster in time...

"Smart and surprising and fast-paced...an excellent book. There were so many small moments in there that I really related to and were just brilliant. (Brearton is) a master at capturing the minutiae of a marriage." — Lisa Regan, author of *Vanishing Girls* *This book was previously published as Breathing Fire, but has been completely revised into this definitive version.

Get The Dark is Always Waiting Now!

Sentenced to life in prison for a crime he didn't commit... Can he be exonerated? After ten years inside a jail cell, Andy Gibbons has abandoned all hope. Resigned himself to the fact that he will spend the rest of his life behind bars. But while Andy may have thrown in the towel, that doesn't mean his wife, Jamie, did. Disillusioned and worn out by the justice system, the Honorable Judge Regan St. Clair is just about to pack in too when a letter from Jamie Gibbons arrives on her desk. A letter that changes everything... Digging deeper, she and a former Special Forces operator named Jake Westley stumble into a frightening underworld of deceit and menace. A world where nothing is as it seems, and no one can be trusted. All the answer these simple question: *Is Andy Gibbons really innocent? Is the price of his freedom worth paying?* **Don't miss this** crime suspense-thriller about a corrupt organization with a sinister agenda that exploits every weakness and every dark corner of the fallible justice system.

Get Unguilty Now!

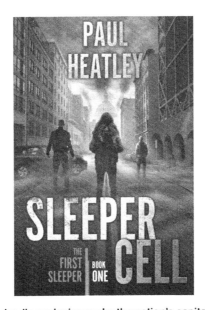

A deadly explosion rocks the nation's capital...
Three seemingly unconnected people – a British ex-
Special Forces operative, an ex-Navy Seal, and a
teenage girl – find themselves under suspicion for the
attack. Soon, they're in the middle of a conspiracy
that threatens to unsettle the entire United States. If
they have any hope to survive the dangerous situation
they've found themselves in, these strangers must
learn to rely on each other, all while the question
remains: Did one of *them* cause the explosion?
**Nefarious organizations arrange themselves
behind the political scenes. The players prepare
their moves. An entire Country hangs in the
balance. Can anyone stop them? Find out in this
adrenaline-pumping action-thriller from bestseller
Paul Heatley.**

Get Sleeper Cell Now!

For all our Thrillers, visit our website.